THE
CYCLOPS
CASE

A JUDGE MARCUS FLAVIUS SEVERUS
MYSTERY IN ANCIENT ROME

ALAN SCRIBNER

Torcular Press

Cover: Fresco of the villa of Livia at Prima Porta

ISBN: 148959731X
ISBN 13: 9781489597311
Library of Congress Control Number: 2013910130
CreateSpace Independent Publishing Platform
North Charleston, South Carolina

Dedication
Ruth and Paul

TABLE OF CONTENTS

   Marcus Flavius Severus: To Himself

PERSONAE

Marcus Flavius Severus - Judge in the Court of the Urban Prefect

Judge Severus' familia

Artemisia - Severus' wife
Aulus, Flavia and Quintus – their 10-year-old, 8-year-old and 2-year-old children
Marcus Flavius Alexander - Severus' freedman and private secretary
Scorpus - slave in charge of the household
Tryphon - slave-valet
Glycon - slave
Galatea - slave
Argos – family dog
Phaon – family cat

Judge Severus' court staff

Quintus Proculus - court clerk
Caius Vulso - centurion in the Urban Cohort
Publius Aelianus Straton - *tesserarius* in the Urban Cohort

Gaius Sempronius Flaccus - judicial assessor

People in Baiae
Gnaeus Avidianus Nepos Cyclops - a Roman General
Publius Bassianus - an agent of the *curiosi* — the imperial secret service

Lucius Herminius - Judge in the Court of Baiae
Eclectus - Judge Herminius' police aide
Marcellus - Judge Herminius' assessor

Titus Vibius Galba - Roman Procurator
Vibia - Galba's daughter
Decimus Ambibulus - Galba's lawyer
Cocceius - Ambibulus' law assistant

Messalina - proprietress of the Blue Oyster Inn in Baiae
Meherdates - a traveling jewelry salesman
Gallicanus - Baiae town councillor
Milo – Baiae building contractor
Titus Mummius - Baiae procurer and brothel owner
Odysseus - namesake of the Homeric hero

People in Puteoli
Floranus, a member of the Puteoli *Vigiles*
Petilius - custodian of a safe-repository in Puteoli
Suren - a priest of Mithra
Zabuttas - priest of the Temple of Mithra in Puteoli
Publius Manilius Carbo - Judge in the Court of Puteoli

People in Rome
Caelius – proprietor of a bookstore on the Vicus Sandalarius

Brennus - an agent of the *curiosi* in Rome
Decius Licinius Valens – *Princeps* of the *curiosi*
Ceionius - a former centurion in the Legion XXII
Deiotariana

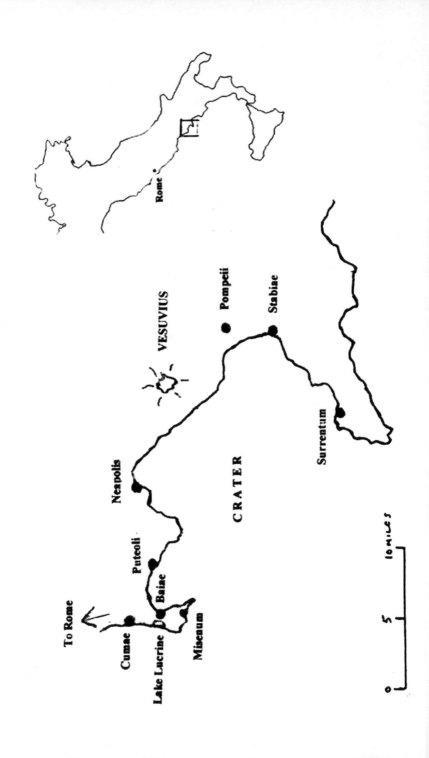

The story is set in the City of Rome and the Bay of Naples – The Crater — in the summer of the year 161 CE during the first year of the reign of the co-Emperors Marcus Aurelius and Lucius Verus, and three years after the case recorded in *Mars the Avenger*.

Major towns surrounding the Crater, and mentioned in this book, are Baiae (pronounced Bye-aye); Neapolis (modern Naples); Puteoli (modern Pozzuoli); Pompeii (destroyed in 79 CE, 82 years before the events in this book).

The Jewish revolt under Hadrian occurred during the years 132-135 CE, almost 30 years before the events in this book.

The Kalends of August is August 1.

The Kalends of September is September 1.

Times of day: The Roman day was divided into 12 day hours starting from sunrise and 12 night hours from sunset. The length of the hour and the onset time of the hour depended on the season since there is more daylight in summer, more night in winter.

For August, close to an equinox, the hours were approximately equal to our hours in length and the first day hour ran from about 6-7 a.m; the first night hour from 6-7 p.m.

For other times specifically mentioned in the book:

The third day hour – 8 - 9 a.m.

The fourth day hour – 9 – 10 a.m.

The sixth day hour – 11a.m. -12 p.m.

The tenth day hour – 3 - 4 p.m.

The fourth night hour – 9 - 10 p.m.

SCROLL I

MARCUS FLAVIUS SEVERUS
TO HIMSELF

Our great historian Tacitus wrote in his *Annals*, "the more I reflect upon events, old or recent, the more I see ironies woven into human affairs." I recall this observation when I reflect upon the murder of General Cyclops and what followed from it. Much as our Stoic and Epicurean philosophers of Nature find an underlying, unseen reality beneath what we think is the world, so too I believe, like Tacitus, there are deeper principles underlying human events. For the Epicureans, the unseen reality is atoms and void, for the Stoics it is the field of energy that generates the matter we actually see. In human affairs, irony may be comparable, informing the overlay of actual events.

I write this *meditatio* 'To Myself' because I set out only to solve the Cyclops case and bring his murderer to justice. But what I really did was meddle in human affairs, stir the underlying reality and precipitate mass murder, which almost included me as a victim. As my wife Artemisia sardonically reminds me — that might have been a fitting irony. Only by a fluke of fate did I survive.

So I have to wonder to what extent were my good intentions the very cause of more evil and therefore to what extent am I responsible? Who really sent all those victims across the river Styx – the murderer or me, or both of us in some sort of mutual dance of law and justice with crime and injustice?

And then there was the war with the Parthian dynasty of Persia to consider. It was precipitated by the death earlier in the year of our long-time emperor Antoninus Pius and the accession of co-emperors Marcus Aurelius and Lucius Verus. Then Persia, as we call that country, or Iran, as the Persians call it, took an opportunity to invade our empire. Long term ambitions and animosities were to be broached once again. And so complementing the clash of infantry and cavalry, of battles and sieges, there was also an espionage and counter-espionage war waged between our imperial secret service – the *curiosi*, and theirs – the *spasaka*, the 'Eye'of the Great King. These became elements of the case I was thrust into.

My involvement started innocently enough in a book-store in Rome, on the Kalends of August, the day before I was to leave for vacation on the Bay of Naples – the Crater.

I

JUDGE SEVERUS HEARS
ABOUT A MURDER

Marcus Flavius Severus, Judge in the Court of the Urban Prefect in the City of Rome, stood on the sidewalk in front of Caelius' bookshop on the Vicus Sandalarius and scanned the list of recently arrived books posted on a column outside the door. The summer sun beat down furiously, smothering the huge concrete and marble city in heat, humidity and smog. The nearby Flavian Amphitheater loomed high above the 4, 5 and 6-story red brick apartment houses crowding the area. Severus took a long sniff on the bag of rose petals in his hand, read a few blurbs describing the new publications, and walked inside.

Since it was the afternoon most people were trying to cool off at the Baths and the bookstore wasn't crowded. Two men browsed quietly among the scrolls arranged in high wooden cubby-holed bookcases, while a few slaves wielding large two-handed fans tried to keep the customers cool and the store from being stifling. Caelius, as usual, sat behind a table near the entrance dressed in an ordinary undyed brown tunic, reading. His store cat, supposedly a menace to any rodent looking for a book to nibble on, was fast asleep on the table. Caelius was slightly stooped by age and slightly disheveled, with a copious white beard shooting out in every direction. But his store was excellently organized, though mainly by his wife.

"*Salve*! Be well, Caelius," called Severus.

"*Salve*! Marcus Flavius Severus," replied the bookseller, as he put down his scroll and rose to greet the judge with a polite kiss.

Severus returned the kiss, and a store slave helped him unwrap his toga and hung it on a hook. Severus wore a white tunic underneath, with narrow reddish-purple stripes – *clavi* – running vertically from shoulder to hem, back and front, displaying a symbol of his Equestrian Class.

The judge was slim and somewhat taller than most, with intelligent gray eyes, a slightly hawkish nose and a sensual mouth. His hair and beard were fashionably short and curled in the style of both the former emperor Antoninus Pius and the new emperor, Marcus Aurelius.

"That's much better," Severus said, fanning the air with his hand. "If there's one law I wish they'd change, it's the one requiring members of the Senatorial and Equestrian Classes to wear their togas on the city streets at all times, no matter how hot it is."

"It's a fitting punishment to compensate for all your upper class privileges," jibed Caelius, with a touch of glee in his voice. "Where's Alexander been?" asked the bookseller. "I haven't seen your private secretary and my best customer for a while."

"The reason is that he's at the Crater. The whole *familia* is going. He went with Artemisia and the children some days ago on the evening boat from Ostia. The slaves drove down in our carriages with all the luggage and the dog and cat. That's why I'm in a good mood, despite this horrible heat. I'm also leaving on vacation. I'm taking the boat from Ostia tomorrow morning."

"The Crater is always lovely," replied Caelius, "and the oysters are always fabulous. Which part are you going to? Not Baiae, to cavort with all those rich playboys and high government officials."

"Certainly not Baiae. Not only do I detest sulphur springs, but I prefer my debauchery in private. No, Caelius, we've taken a villa near Neapolis. We decided on Neapolis because this is the year for the *Sebasta* Greek Games. There should be some interesting athletic and musical contests. Apart from that, we plan to read, relax and swim, and I hope to do some star-gazing. I even bought a new *diopter* sighting instrument to help focus on and observe the stars and planets. Also since Neapolis is a Greek city, we can wear Greek clothing there – no togas.

"Of course," added Severus slyly, "Artemisia and I have to spend at least one day and one night in Baiae. After all, it is supposed to be the greatest pleasure city in the world."

"Baiae is as sensational this year as ever," replied Caelius. "Did you hear about the murder?"

"No. What murder?"

"Didn't you see it in the Daily Acts this morning? That notorious one-eyed general, General Cyclops, was found murdered on the beach in Baiae. Here, I'll get my copy of the article."

Caelius rummaged through the scrolls and tablets piled on his table and pulled out the tablet with the news that his slave had copied from the news boards in the Old Forum. He opened the wooden cover to the first waxed page.

"It says that he was found on the beach yesterday morning. There was a dagger through his good eye."

"Incredible!" exclaimed Severus. "The murderer must have a taste for Homer and *The Odyssey* to stab someone named Cyclops through his eye. Did the *Vigiles* catch this Odysseus?"

"It doesn't say," replied Caelius, flipping to the next page of the tablet. "Maybe there'll be more in tomorrow's Daily Acts. Today's just gives a basic obituary. Born Gnaeus Avidianus Nepos, after he lost an eye in battle and won a field commission, he proudly added 'Cyclops' to his cognomen. There's a long list of medals and campaigns. It looks almost as if he'd been with every one of the twenty-eight legions. His last field command, it says, was as commanding legate of the legion XII Fulminata on the Persian frontier. That was a few years ago, though, when there was peace there. Not like what's been going on for the last few months with the Persian invasion." Caelius closed the tablet and pushed it back into the pile on his table.

"It sounds like an interesting case," remarked the judge. "I'm sure I'll hear much more about it while I'm at the Crater."

Severus then wandered down the aisle between the bookcases glancing at titles written on reds tags dangling from scroll ends and opening a scroll here and there to read. A slave with a two-handed fan followed him at a discrete distance stirring the air. At the end of an hour browsing in both the Latin and Greek wings of the store, he had selected three books.

At the front desk, he handed Caelius a set of scrolls. "It's Lucian's new *fabula, A True History,* he calls it. And he says here at the very beginning that just like athletes need relaxation as well as strenuous training, we all need relaxing reading as well as serious reading, so I'm going to follow his advice and take this book to read while on vacation."

"Ah yes, Lucian of Samosata," replied Caelius. "My favorite satirist. I've already read it. And *You'll* definitely like it. It has a war between inhabitants of the Moon against inhabitants of the Sun over colonizing Venus. The Moon-ites ride giant vultures for their cavalry, while the Sun-ites ride giant winged ants. And they both have allies from the stars…."

"Giant ants?" interjected Severus, his face lighting up. "The Moon, the Sun, the stars all inhabited? Now I really want to read this."

"It's all fantasy by Lucian and can't be a true history, of course," commented Caelius. "People living elsewhere in the Cosmos — on the Sun, the Moon and the stars? Is that possible? The Sun, after all, is a ball of fire."

"I don't know about the Sun," replied Severus, always happy to engage in conversation about one of his pet interests, "but you certainly know that Lucretius

and the Epicureans think the Universe is infinite. And
if infinite, they conclude there must be an infinite number of other Earths, and infinite Suns, Moons and stars.
And if there are infinite other Earths, then there must be
other inhabitants. Like Metrodoros of Chios said, it is
as absurd to think that in an infinite Cosmos the Earth
is the only populated world as it is to think that in an
entire field sown with wheat only one grain will grow.
So maybe the Sun, Moon and the stars are inhabited. We
really don't know. But evidently Lucian believes in an
infinite Universe and in fact, Caelius, that's how I think
about the Universe, even without Lucian."

The bookseller raised his bushy eyebrows and pondered a few moments.

Severus then handed him another set of scrolls —
a Greek *fabula*, *Callirhoe* by Chariton of Aphrodisias.
"Artemisia asked me to get her a good historical story.
How is this one?"

"I liked it and my wife loved it," replied Caelius.
"It takes place during the Peloponnesian war, about 500
years ago, after Athens attacked Syracuse, and goes all
over the world, to Egypt, Babylon, Persia. But it's the
usual story of beautiful youths falling in love, then being kept apart by changes of fortune, adventures, pirates,
shipwrecks, lots of ups and downs, everything from eggs
to apples. At the end, of course, they happily find each
other again. It's well written and you'll both like it."

"I also found this for her," said Severus, handing
Caelius a codex style book with papyrus pages – a beautiful illustrated edition of *On Birds* by Boethus. "Among
her numerous interests, Artemisia loves birds and she's
going to enjoy matching the birds she sees outside to

the pictures in the book and vice versa. And this codex will be much more convenient than a scroll for flipping through pages and keeping open for reference."

"The Lucian and the Chariton are six sesterces apiece," said Caelius as he moved the counters of his abacus to total the purchase. "and the Boethus — a beautiful book, isn't it — unfortunately is a lot more. 100 sesterces."

"100 sesterces!" exclaimed the judge with surprise. "It's not that old or rare, is it?"

"It's old enough and rare enough, judge," replied Caelius quickly. "Do you know the prices of rare books nowadays? I recently sold a first edition of volume II of Vergil's *Aeneid* for 2,000 sesterces. Of course, it belonged to Vergil himself, so the cost was..."

The judge gave Caelius a suspicious look. "Are you sure you're not doing more in the back rooms than publishing books?" said Severus only half in jest.

"Really, judge," replied Caelius seeing Severus' expression. "It wasn't a fake first edition. I have it on good authority. It belonged to Vergil himself."

Severus was only half convinced. "I'll take the Boethus anyway. Put the books on my account, Caelius."

The bookseller totaled the purchase on his abacus and figured in the 1% sales tax, the proceeds of which were dedicated to the military treasury. "It comes to 112 sesterces. 113 with the tax." He wrapped the codex in cheap wrapping papyrus, tied it with a string, and handed it to the judge. The scrolls he placed in a *capsa*, a cylindrical case for carrying book rolls and closed the cover. Caelius then took the judge's toga off the hook.

"Here, let me help you wind this back on. It will keep you nice and warm outside."

Severus cracked a smile.

"Have a good vacation," said Caelius.

"I'm sure I will," answered Severus..

The judge walked back into the heat, wondering who had killed General Cyclops in that way, and why.

II

THE JUDGE GETS AN ASSIGNMENT

"*Euge*! very good," exclaimed Artemisia when she saw Severus' javelin hit near the target area circled on the ground. "A few more throws and maybe you'll hit it."

"A few more throws," remarked Severus as he rubbed his arm, "and I won't be able to throw for the next few days."

It was the morning after Severus' arrival at the villa outside Neapolis. The sun was bright and warm and the air clean and fresh. After his favorite breakfast of white bread soaked in milk and honey, Judge Severus, his wife Artemisia and the two older children, Aulus 10 and Flavia 8, dashed outside to a field behind the villa for morning sports. They were accompanied by their large black guard dog, Argos, who loved to run alongside during the warm-up races, barking excitedly while the children screamed happily. When the javelin throwing began, they were joined by Alexander, Severus' freedman and private secretary and by Tryphon, his slave-valet.

Another of their slaves, Galatea, kept her eyes on two-year-old Quintus pulling a small wheeled crocodile, its mouth opening and closing as it moved. The family cat, Phaon, gave the whole scene a wide berth and a suspicious glare.

Alexander, Tryphon and Aulus wore short athletic tunics, while Artemisia and Flavia wore the traditional garb of competitors in women's events — a short tunic ending above the knees with the right shoulder bare. It complemented Artemisia's slim and graceful figure. Her long dark hair was worn loose.

Severus held the Greek attitude that men should compete in sports in the nude, regarding the Roman practice of wearing clothes as decadent. Nevertheless he wore a tunic in this Roman family setting.

Artemisia stepped behind the throwing line, placed the javelin thong carefully over her middle and index fingers, took a deep breath, hefted the shaft, and made her run. Though an Athenian, she admired the Spartan way of raising girls and threw the javelin using the Spartan throwing-whoop — "*a-la-la-la-la*". The javelin went off to the right, evoking her expletive — "*merda*! shit." Severus watched only her and countered her epithet by smiling and mouthing to himself the word *bella*, beautiful.

Next the children threw their lighter javelins at a closer target. Argos retrieved their weapons and brought them back to the Flavia and Aulus, while everyone cheered him on with words of encouragement and praise.

Alexander and Tryphon both tried to look very professional when they tested the feel of their javelins and made practice runs. But neither was convincing.

Alexander was too slight of build and somewhat too gawky. His strength lay in his mind, which was filled with facts and knowledge. People said of Alexander that he was more excited by an interesting fact than most people were by a victory of the Greens in the chariot races. Tryphon was just too old and out of shape. They both missed by wide margins.

As Judge Severus made another run, a figure in military dress emerged from the back portico of the house.

"If you threw like that and were in my cohort," called the soldier, "I'd have you all put on rations of barley."

"Vulso!" exclaimed Severus when he saw his aide. "What are you doing here? I thought you were in Rome."

Caius Vulso, a centurion in Rome's Urban Cohort, and a veteran of a 20-year career with the legions, strode briskly onto the throwing field. He carried his centurion's vinewood swagger stick in one hand and a large multi-leaved wooden tablet in the other. Vulso was tall and strong and confident, with chiseled features and a short, trimmed military beard. He had an air of controlled brutality about him, but he was very smart and had educated himself. He was a formidable person and Severus relied upon Vulso both to advise him and to intimidate others. Vulso exchanged greeting kisses with everyone and turned to the judge.

"Have you heard about the murder of General Cyclops in Baiae?" he asked directly.

"Yes. A dagger through his good eye. What of it?"

"The Urban Prefect has assigned the Cyclops case to you." Vulso handed Severus the wooden tablet. "He wants you to solve it."

The judge took the tablet. "He does?" A look of uncertainty passed over Severus' face. "But what about the local judge? There must be one on the case already. And what about my authority? We're more than 100 miles from Rome and the jurisdiction of the Prefect of the City of Rome doesn't extend beyond the 100th milestone."

Vulso shrugged his shoulders. "I was summoned to the Praefectura building three days ago at the first hour. The prefect himself saw me. He said he's sorry to interrupt your vacation, but it can't be helped. The case is of concern to the emperor, the army, and the *curiosi*."

"The *curiosi*?" exclaimed Severus. "What does the imperial secret service have to do with this?"

"You're to read that," replied Vulso pointing to the tablet in Severus' hand. "The prefect said it will explain everything. As for the 100-mile jurisdiction," continued Vulso, "the prefect thought of that too."

"What did he say?"

"He gave me a document temporarily assigning you to the case as assessor to Judge Lucius Herminius — he's the judge in Baiae currently in charge of the investigation. It will preserve some legal form, but you're to be in charge."

"But that document's a sham. The city prefect in Baiae won't stand for such an intrusion into his court's jurisdiction, even if this Judge Herminius does. A judge always chooses his own assessor."

"As I said," replied Vulso with a laugh, "the prefect has an answer. He just told me that if anyone complains too much about something technical like the 100-mile limit, the answer is..." Vulso completed the sentence by holding his middle finger up in the air in an obscene gesture. "That's how the prefect phrased it to me, judge," the centurion explained, "and I'm merely reporting his instructions, gesture for gesture."

Severus laughed. "I suppose I'll have to be somewhat more diplomatic in conveying that message." The judge thought for a moment. "I'll have to get my court clerk and my own judicial assessor from Rome for the..."

"I've already seen to it," interrupted the centurion. "Proculus and Flaccus are coming by boat and will be here tomorrow morning or the next day. I've also sent for Straton to help me in the police and undercover work, so we'll be at full strength.

"Also an advantage of having the government and the *curiosi* involved is that we have a *diploma* to use the couriers and vehicles of the Imperial Post, the *cursus publicus*, at any time. Our *diploma* also includes free meals and lodgings at any of their way-stations."

"Excellent, Vulso," said the judge turning to his secretary. "Alexander, send a message to this Judge Herminius in Baiae. I want to meet with him in his chambers there tomorrow."

"As for now," concluded the judge, holding up the wooden tablet, "I'm anxious to read this."

III

A MESSAGE FROM THE PREFECT
AND THE EPIC OF THE ODYSSEY

After an early dinner, Severus and Artemisia went for an evening stroll along the country roads, while Alexander gave Vulso a brief tour of the summer house.

The villa was a two-level building, colonnaded front and back. The slender columns were smooth and round and painted a soft green a third of the way up then white and fluted up to their simple Doric capitals. Inside the front door, a vestibule led to the large common area — the atrium. At the back of the atrium, behind a curtain was the *tablinum* – a working area with desk and chairs – and at the back of that was a curtain leading to a pleasant open air peristyle. The peristyle had a flower pool in the center and a balcony overlooking it from the second floor. Behind and around the atrium and peristyle were bedrooms, a library, the dining room and kitchen, while the top floor housed more bedrooms. The walls were decorated with frescoes, mostly seascapes in soft pastel greens and blues or pastoral landscapes in greens and browns, while the marble floors were colorful mosaics with geometric designs.

One special feature of the villa was a *sphaeristerium* — a ball court. "The household," explained Alexander, "divides up into teams to play 'Over the Line' or sometimes a few of us play 'Intercept' or just have a catch." Vulso idly kicked a large green air filled ball against the ball court wall. "Doctors say ball playing is good for your health," added Alexander didactically.

Behind the house was a small shaded garden centered around a fishpond. The villa was fronted by a cool grove of umbrella pines, split by a driveway which led to a dirt road which, after a brief walk past one other villa, led down to the beach.

"You can hear the sea and even smell it in the air," said Alexander filling his lungs, "and the sky at night is so clear you can see the colors of the stars. Living in Rome, with all its smog, almost makes me forget what the night sky really looks like."

The house-slaves were lighting the oil lamps in the library when Alexander and Vulso came in. Severus and Artemisia returned from their walk a few minutes later and settled on white-cushioned reading couches. They both wore plain blue tunics, Severus' sea blue, Artemisia's sky blue, while Vulso had on his red military tunic. Alexander was dressed more elegantly, in a dark green tunic with red *clavi*, a red belt and a yellow headband. The judge waited until the slaves put fruit and wine on the table between the couches, lit the incense burners, and left the room, closing the doors behind them. The pungent smell of myrrh wafted through the room. The judge took a sip of wine and began.

"It's more complicated than we thought. There have been two murders, not one."

"Two murders?" asked Vulso. "Who else besides General Cyclops?"

"Let me begin with Cyclops," replied the judge.

"According to the report, it seems that the general wasn't just vacationing in Baiae. He was *persona non grata* in Rome and had been advised to leave the City. It seems he fell into disfavor with the government because of his too vociferous opposition to Emperor Antoninus' peace policy with Persia."

Vulso snorted. "Well, the Persian invasion a few months ago has invalidated that policy."

"Yes, unfortunately. But this happened a few years ago," continued the judge, "when there was peace. You may remember that rumors were flying all over Rome then that the Persians had mobilized their army and were intending to invade Armenia, which is under our protection. Apparently military intelligence on the frontier and *curiosi* spies inside Persia had gotten wind of King Vologases' plans and alerted the generals in Rome.

"Out of the high-level meetings on how to handle the threat, there arose two factions. One, led by the bureaucracy, favored a diplomatic effort to resolve the crisis, while a second faction, led by the army, was for war. Cyclops was one of the leaders of the war party."

Severus paused and took a sip of wine.

"The generals argued that the Persians should be allowed to attack and then we could crush them. Emperor Trajan's lesson fifty years ago, when he sacked their capital at Ctesiphon and captured the Great King's family and his Golden Throne, should now be re-taught. It was always the army's view that Emperor Hadrian's policy of giving up Mesopotamia and returning it to the Persians was a mistake — a signal to them of appeasement and weakness. The army argued that the Persians only understood force. But Antoninus decided otherwise. We all know his oft-proclaimed policy that he would rather save a single citizen than slay a thousand foes…"

"A dubious sentiment," interjected Vulso.

"I think it's beautiful," retorted Artemisia.

"In any event," continued Severus, "at least as a first step, Antoninus opted to use diplomatic channels and sent a personal letter to Vologases, letting him know we were aware of his plans and warning him in the strongest terms not to invade Armenia. He also moved reinforcements to the border, pointedly refused to return the Golden Throne and threatened all-out war if they persisted. As we all know, there was no war then. The Persians backed down."

"This is all ironic now," commented Vulso. "The peace party has been proved wrong, and the desk generals were too sure of themselves. Look at what's happening. A whole legion massacred, a fortress captured, and the capital of Armenia about to fall.

"But we'll turn the tide," he predicted confidently. "A few crack legions from the German frontier will probably be sent to the East — they will take care of the Persians. The eastern legions are sapped by too much luxurious living. A dose of European backbone will be the cure. We'll sack Ctesiphon again to boot, mark my words."

"Do you think they invaded now," asked Alexander, " because of the death of Antoninus and the accession of Marcus Aurelius?"

"Absolutely!" answered Vulso. "The Persians know that our new emperor is popularly known as 'the philosopher' and they are testing him. They didn't give up their plans; they were just waiting for old Antoninus to die. And then they didn't waste any time. How long did it take them to invade after Marcus' accession, a month or two?"

"I hope you're right about the outcome, Vulso," commented Artemisia with a worried frown. "Rumors are rife that the whole East is threatened. There's panic throughout Syria. Some people are already preparing to evacuate Antioch. The Greeks are calling it another Xerxes invasion."

"Over-reacting as usual," shot back Vulso. "Not only the rumors but 'greeklings' and orientals as well."

Artemisia returned a dirty look. Though a Roman citizen, she had been born and grew up in Athens and was of Greek heritage. She disliked anyone using the all too common ethnic slur 'greekling'. "It will take your European legions at least a half a year to get there, maybe more. What happens until then?"

Vulso looked grim. "The other eastern legions will just have to hold."

"In any event," continued Severus, reverting to the subject at hand, "at the time we're talking about Cyclops wouldn't accept the decision to use diplomacy and continued to agitate for war. And his agitation became too embarrassing after Antoninus opted for the peace policy. So he was told to take a long absence from active duty.

That's why he was at the Crater. However, according to the prefect, because of the current emergency he was about to be recalled and given an important command in the war."

The judge drained his wine glass and then refilled it. "The importance of this for our purposes is that the general's outspoken and even insubordinate conduct made him a person of interest to the imperial secret service. The *curiosi* examined his mail, had him followed and interviewed friends and people he associated with about Cyclops' loyalty to the emperor. It wasn't obtrusive — or so the *curiosi* claim — but they wanted to know what Cyclops was up to. Evidently the *curiosi* always suspect there are plots against the emperor and anyone opposing imperial policy too strongly is an automatic suspect."

"Now," said Severus with emphasis, "listen to this. The surveillance didn't stop when the general left Rome. Even while Cyclops was in Baiae, he was followed by an agent of the *curiosi*, a man named Publius Bassianus. And Bassianus was found dead the morning after Cyclops himself was killed. He had been staying at a place called the Blue Oyster Inn in Baiae and was found floating face down in a fish pond behind the inn.

"Though it could have been an accident — he could have tripped, hit his head, and fallen into the pool and drowned — the *curiosi* think their agent was murdered and they're furious about it. They care more about the death of Bassianus than about the murder of Cyclops. And that, it seems, is why I've been assigned to the case. The *curiosi* won't have any local judge meddling in *curiosi* affairs. They want someone from Rome."

"Maybe Cyclops and the *curiosi* agent were murdered by Persian spies," ventured Vulso. "They have their own internal security and spy organization too, much older than ours. It's called the *spasaka* — The 'Eye' of the Great King. I'm sure they knew that Cyclops was one of the leaders of the war party and could anticipate he would be recalled to the colors and sent against them. They had reason to want him dead."

"There's no point speculating, Vulso," replied Severus. "We don't know enough yet. For all we know, Cyclops could have been killed in a lover's quarrel and Bassianus could have had a heart attack. We'll find out the facts and circumstances of both deaths when I talk to Judge Herminius in Baiae tomorrow and read the police reports and court files. There may be suspects already."

"Now," said Severus a little more happily, "let's call in the children and the slaves, have some more food and wine, and the whole *familia* will listen to Alexander tell us a story. What have you chosen for tonight, Alexander?"

Alexander rose from his couch, went to his room, and returned with a cylindrical scroll box. The household slaves brought in stools and benches so they could also sit and hear the after-dinner story. The children settled on couches with their parents. Even Argos and Phaon came in to listen, Argos curling up on the floor while Phaon sprang onto the couch next to Flavia. When everyone was settled, Alexander pulled out a scroll and placed it by his side on the couch.

"Tonight," he said with a smile, "I've chosen something appropriate, perhaps even helpful for the investigation. I'm going to tell the story of Odysseus' adventures."

Vulso chuckled. "He thinks cases can be solved by reading old legends. I'm tired and I'm going to bed."

When polite 'good nights' were exchanged and Vulso left the library, Alexander began the story of Odysseus' ten-year journey from Troy to his home in Ithaca. In his own words, but spiced with excerpts in the beautiful metered poetry of Homer, Alexander told a tale that was second nature to his listeners. Everyone had read it, recited it, or heard it countless times since childhood. But it was still absorbing. Like hearing a loved and familiar piece of music, it didn't matter how many times one had heard it before.

In the dim light of the oil lamps, Alexander told how Odysseus set out for home after the long war against Troy had ended, and about the adventures which delayed his return to his wife Penelope. He related how Odysseus' ship was caught in a storm and blown to the land of the Lotus Eaters where the sweet lotus food produced forgetfulness; and then how Odysseus and his shipmates came to the country of the Cyclopes, one-eyed monsters who devoured his men until wily Odysseus devised the scheme of getting the Cyclops Polyphemus drunk and poked out his eye with a sharpened stake. Then on to the Island of Aeolus, Keeper of the Winds, where a departing gift, a bag enclosing the winds themselves, was opened by greedy sailors hoping to find treasure, but instead unleashed winds that blew them out to sea again. He told how they then encountered the Lastrygonians, cannibals of immense size, who shattered eleven of Odysseus' ships with huge stones. On the Island of Aeaea, the sorceress Circe turned Odysseus' men into swine and entertained Odysseus with a year of amusement and pleasure.

Then there were the Isles of the Sirens, whose enticing call Odysseus averted by stuffing wax in his ears when sailing by. There was the dangerous passage between the rock and the whirlpool, Scylla and Charybdis, and the landfall on the Island of the nymph Calypso, who kept Odysseus with her for seven years with promises of immortality and eternal youth.

And Alexander told how Odysseus' yearning drove him once more in quest of his home, and how, after further adventures and the loss of all his crew, he was rescued by the Princess Nausicaa and the Phaeacians. And finally, Alexander recounted how Odysseus reached Ithaca after his twenty-year absence. There, his wife Penelope had for years resisted the marriage demands of suitors who claimed her husband was dead, by weaving a shroud during the days and unraveling her work during the nights. And then Odysseus returned in the guise of a beggar, unrecognized except by his old dog, Argos. At this, Severus' dog Argos perked up his ears and wagged his tail once or twice, while everyone noticed and smiled at his attentiveness. Alexander then continued the story of Odysseus' return, telling how he enlisted the aid of his son Telemachus and in a climactic scene slew the suitors with arrows from the powerful bow which none but Odysseus could draw.

"I hope," commented Judge Severus when the story was ended, "that the murderer of General Cyclops won't be quite that formidable."

SCROLL II

IV

JUDGE HERMINIUS

Baiae was Rome's most famous resort. A town of hot sulphur baths and seaside attractions, it catered to the ailments of the sick and the pleasures of the sound. It's beauty was proverbial. "No other bay on earth outshines lovely Baiae," said Horace. Its curving shores, sparkling waters, cool green myrtle groves and mineral springs basked in the clear air and bright sky of "cloudless Baiae." Imperial palaces and luxurious villas clustered about the "golden shore of the Goddess of Love." "Though I were to extol Baiae with a thousand verses," said Martial, "I could never extol Baiae worthily enough."

Baiae was the "Bay of Luxury." It was also the "Bay of Immorality." Seneca called it the "Inn of Vice" and felt compelled to leave the day after he arrived. Varro noted that in Baiae young men came out as girls, while old men came out as little boys, and Martial wrote of the common stories where men come for a thermal cure and leave with a broken heart, and women arrive as Penelope and leave as Helen of Troy. Orgies, flirtations, dinner parties, drinking parties, beach parties, villa parties, boating parties, musical entertainments and concerts were the life of Baiae.

Fittingly, Baiae's most renowned product, after sex and gambling, was a culinary delicacy. Its delicious oysters were grown in artificial beds in a local lake, which aptly was named for the vast profits reaped from their sale; Lake Lucrine — the Lake of Lucre.

At dawn the next day, Severus, along with his private secretary Alexander and police aide Vulso, were picked up at his vacation villa outside Neapolis by a fast four-horse, four wheeled covered carriage of the Imperial Post. They were driven along the highway, through the 1/3 of a mile long tunnel cut through the Posillipo hills, past Puteoli and then on to Baiae. They made good time, traveling the eight miles in little over an hour, and were brought safely if sometimes jarringly to the white-colonnaded courthouse in the Forum of Baiae. Waiting court-slaves held the hem of the judge's toga as he descended from the carriage. Judge Herminius came outside, exchanged a polite greeting kiss, and personally escorted Judge Severus to his chambers.

At Herminius' suggestion, court-slaves helped the judges remove their judicial togas and Judge Severus was invited to recline on a couch. Both magistrates wore the symbols of their status in society as members of the Equestrian Class: a white tunic with the narrow reddish-purple vertical *clavi*, black "patrician shoes" and a simple gold ring.

Severus admired an elegant linen tapestry with a hunting scene hanging on one wall. Portrait paintings of the senior and junior emperors, Marcus Aurelius and Lucius Verus, were displayed on another wall of the judge's chambers.

Court slaves quietly placed a platter of fresh lake oysters on the table between the couches and filled drinking glasses with a snow-chilled Greek white wine, while Severus made himself comfortable and looked over the local judge.

Herminius was a thin, distinguished looking man. His hair and beard were half-gray and half-black, like a mixture of salt and pepper. A slightly ironic manner and quick smile made him appear intelligent. His speech was erudite. But he bore himself a little too properly for Severus' tastes and seemed overly correct and formal.

Severus devoured three oysters in quick succession and drained the wine glass. "May I compliment you on your selection of refreshments," he said politely. "The oysters are wonderful. And so is the wine."

"The selection," replied Herminius as a slave refilled Severus' glass from a wine cask on the table, "is a local tradition. But the wine is from my cellar." He turned the label on the cask in Severus' direction. "It's a five-year-old Chian, although perhaps you know from the taste."

"I suspected a Chian," replied Severus, "but I'm not an expert. I do know, however, that these oysters are delicious." He emphasized his point by eating another.

The conversation continued politely, but awkwardly, until the oysters were gone and the slaves cleared away the platters and departed, leaving the two magistrates alone with the wine and a bowl of grapes and apples.

Herminius' court clerk placed a court file on the table in front of his judge and also left. Then Judge Herminius broke the silence.

"I understand," he said with a chill in his voice, "that you are to relieve me of the investigation into the murder of General Cyclops."

Severus looked and sounded apologetic. "It was not my idea, Judge Herminius. I was in the area on vacation and the Urban Prefect assigned me to the case without my knowledge or approval. I would prefer not to have it and I regret the embarrassment caused by this irregularity. I would like to work amicably with you and I would hope that you do not hold my intercession in the case against me." Severus hoped his little prepared speech would end the matter. It almost did.

"I don't really mind," replied Herminius with a touch of malice, "if the authorities in Rome wish to clean up a mess with which they are undoubtedly more familiar than I. But it does escape me how a judge from Rome has any jurisdiction in Baiae. We are, I believe, beyond the 100th milestone from the Capital."

"I'm baffled by that too, Judge Herminius. In fact I raised the same objection when I heard of my assignment. The authorities in Rome, however, seem to think that my technical appointment as your assessor for this case will satisfy the jurisdictional question. Technically you're still in charge."

"That's a mere sham, Judge Severus," replied Herminius. "I was told you are to be in actual charge. Besides, who gave the prefect in Rome any authority to appoint my judicial assessor? I already have an assessor and, as you well know, it is a judge's prerogative to choose the person who will sit with him and help him decide cases."

"Perhaps you can ask the Bureau of Judicial Affairs in Rome for an advisory opinion. They might issue an Imperial Rescript directed to the legal point."

"The prefect of my court is drawing up the documents, though I suppose, the Cyclops case will be long concluded by the time Judicial Affairs decides you have no jurisdiction."

"Until then..." Herminius hesitated, "I have no choice but to cooperate with you."

Severus breathed a sigh of relief and Herminius' thin smile showed he was mollified by Severus' deferential attitude. He would be compliant, at least for the time being.

"That is an amicable solution," said Severus. "So perhaps now you can fill me in on the details of the murder. I understand General Cyclops was stabbed in the good eye like the legendary Cyclops, Polyphemus, but I have no other facts about the homicide."

"He was indeed. And also like the mythical Cyclops he was drunk. The general was killed on the Kalends of August. He was found on the beach by late night carousers, in the area of New Baiae known as 'Nero's Pond'. When the *Vigiles* arrived, the body was still warm and he reeked of wine. An almost empty wine skin lay on the sand next to him. The dagger was still in his eye."

Herminius opened the court file, but spoke without glancing at the documents inside.

"The *Vigiles* interviewed people on the beach and in the vicinity, but learned nothing. I interviewed the slaves in Cyclops' villa and took written affidavits from them. They said the general had left in the late afternoon, they thought to go gambling at the Blue Oyster Inn, as he did almost every night. He returned an hour before midnight, laughing, singing songs and celebrating. They guessed he had won at the gambling tables. He took a shower-bath, changed his clothes, called for wine and a writing case, then retired to his room.

"About midnight, the general came out, drunk and singing an obscene song. He called for a lantern and left the villa, taking a full wine skin, his writing case and a rolled up sheet of papyrus with him. He never returned. The lantern and writing case were found on the sand besides the wine skin, but the papyrus was gone, likely blown away."

"That's quite odd, isn't it?" commented Severus. "Why would he take papyrus and pen to the beach in the middle of the night?"

Herminius shrugged his shoulders. "I have no idea."

"Are there any suspects?" asked Severus.

"There are leads," replied Judge Herminius circumspectly. "For instance, the slaves said that in the afternoon Cyclops had a visit from a traveling jeweler by the name of Meherdates."

"Meherdates!" exclaimed Severus. "A Persian?"

"The name is Persian," replied Herminius, "but people at the inn where Meherdates stayed said he claimed he was from Syria. In the East, one encounters many Persian names in the Roman provinces bordering Persia. But whatever he is, his meeting with the general is suspicious. Cyclops' slaves said that they heard shouting and yelling from the room where the general received the jeweler. Then Meherdates was angrily shown out, the slaves receiving instructions never to let him in again. Not long afterwards Cyclops left the villa."

Herminius took a papyrus sheet from the court file and handed it to Judge Severus. "This is a painting of Meherdates, made by our police artist from descriptions given by the slaves and by the people at the Blue Oyster, where Meherdates was staying."

"Is that the same Blue Oyster where Cyclops went gambling?"

"It is. And that also is suspicious, because Meherdates had only been there for a few days and, though he told the management that he intended to stay for two weeks, he left abruptly early the next morning, at dawn."

Severus looked at the painting. It showed a turbaned older man with a heavy black, eastern-style beard, cut square at the bottom. He handed the painting back to Herminius.

"We haven't been able to find the jeweler," continued Herminius. "Since he told people at the inn that he was touring the Crater area trying to sell jewels to rich vacationers, I've had the *Vigiles* check various inns in the area and in nearby towns, in Misenum, Cumae, Puteoli, Neapolis, even as far as Surrentum. But he seems to have disappeared."

"Are there any other leads?" asked Severus. "What about women?"

"There were women in his life," answered Herminius, "although I wouldn't categorize them as suspects. For instance, Cyclops was apparently enamored of two Syrian sisters, touring singers and dancing girls, who perform obscenely in public at the Blue Oyster and privately at parties. According to Cyclops' slaves, they sometimes spent nights with him."

Herminius took a sip of wine. "Also according to the general's slaves, he acquired a mistress while he was in Baiae. A young girl named Vibia. She is the daughter of T. Vibius Galba, a Procurator with the Bureau of the Treasury in Rome. They're vacationing in Baiae and have the villa next to Cyclops'.

"For completeness of the court records, I interviewed her. She is flirtatious and uncontrollable, a typical product to my mind of high-living and big city ways. Cyclops' slaves alleged she spent many nights in the general's bed, but she denied it when I questioned her. She does however acknowledge having gone boating with him on several occasions. Officially, of course, I accept her word over the word of slaves."

"I understand perfectly," replied Severus. "I'll have a talk with her."

"It would undoubtedly be a waste of time." Judge Herminius paused. "Of course," he continued, "there is always the possibility that General Cyclops was killed by some criminal or robber. There are gangs in the hills, you know, and sometimes they sneak into town to commit crimes."

Judge Severus drained his wine glass and leaned over the table to grasp the wine jug and refill his glass.

"You've mentioned the Blue Oyster Inn several times. What sort of a place is it?"

"Disreputable," replied Herminius with an edge of contempt in his voice. "It's rather a large establishment, specializing in eating, drinking, gambling and sex, a combination hotel, restaurant, tavern, dance hall, gambling house and brothel. Baiae is the perfect location for it. It's run by a woman named Messalina, a former dancing girl herself, who made a reputation and a lot of money in her younger years. I've met her, of course, since the Blue Oyster has been the scene of a number of incidents which required judicial scrutiny. I am told, however, that the dice are not loaded."

"I understand," said Severus carefully, "that there was a mysterious death there recently. A man named Publius Bassianus."

Herminius gave Severus a shrewd look.

"There's nothing mysterious about it. He was murdered."

"How do you know that?"

"The death was investigated by the *Vigiles* and I was informed about it. He was found drowned in the Blue Oyster's fish pond the morning after General Cyclops' murder. According to the police doctor, he had a wound on the front of his head, caused either by a fall or by being struck with a heavy object. The *Vigiles* searched the area and found a large rock in the bushes around the pool and the rock had fresh bloodstains on it. So it seems likely that he was knocked unconscious with the rock and then deliberately drowned in the pool."

"Caught between the rock and the whirlpool, was he? Between Scylla and Charybdis?" said Severus with a wry smile.

"What do you mean by that?"

"Cyclops was killed like his namesake in the Odyssey," mused Severus. "The way Bassianus died…."

"O, you mean the same person who killed General Cyclops killed Bassianus, a lunatic perhaps who is killing in the manner of the Odyssey stories. How clever of you, Judge Severus, to think of that."

Severus held up his hand, as if backing off. "Just a speculation, Judge Herminius. We don't really have the evidence yet to draw that conclusion. But it's possible. In any event, did the police doctor make an estimate of the time when the killing of Bassianus occurred?"

"He thinks Bassianus had been in the pool most of the night. So he was killed the night before he was found. We have, however, not been able to discover who he was, where he came from, what he was doing at the Blue Oyster Inn, where he went during the day, or who would want to kill him. No one at the inn knew anything about him.

"So the only question I have for you, Judge Severus, is — how do *you* know about him?"

Severus considered the question for a long moment. "He was an agent of the *curiosi* and he was assigned to spy on General Cyclops."

Herminius considered the answer for an equally long moment. "It's your problem now," he said finally, as if he was no longer interested in the whole affair. He then changed the subject.

"You may wish to spend a few days here in Baiae while conducting the investigation. I will provide a room for you to work in and a courtroom if you need to conduct official hearings. I will also arrange a place to stay, if you like."

"Thank you for your offer, Judge Herminius," replied Severus. "I'll let you know when I need the facilities. But I intend to spend as little time as possible in a stuffy courtroom wrapped in a suffocating toga. As for lodgings," he added as an idea flashed through his mind, "I think I'll take a room at the Blue Oyster Inn. After all," he explained lamely in response to the look of disapproval that passed over Judge Herminius' face, "it should be investigated."

V

THE BLUE OYSTER INN

The Empire was filled with inns. Travelers from the poorest vagabond to the businessman on an expense account, from wealthy tourists to government officials could all find lodgings in the roadside *deversoria* that followed the great network of paved highways and marbled towns that criss-crossed the Empire from Britannia to Persia, from Germania to Aegyptus. The inns varied from dirty shacks to well-appointed villas, but they all had bad reputations. Some were even dangerous, where it was said the traveler took greater risks inside from the owners than outside from the elements and highwaymen. But in every inn a traveler could be sure to find three things: a bed, something to eat and drink, and a bed partner.

The Blue Oyster Inn was no different. But it was a four story country house instead of a shack, its beds stuffed with goose feathers instead of reeds, its fare roasts, pheasants and oysters rather than gruel. And its women were beautiful and accomplished entertainers rather than just the wife of the proprietor or an over-worked slave. Then there was the gambling, music and dancing at the Blue Oyster. A variety of dice and board games constantly absorbed the passions and money of gamblers, while lascivious singing and dancing girls absorbed the passions and money of the rest. For the vacationer, the Blue Oyster provided a night on the town, a temptation difficult to resist, and another allurement along with the torchlight boating, beach revelries and villa parties which were the daily fare of social life in Baiae.

Severus, Alexander and Vulso were shown to rooms on the third floor of the inn. The first floor was devoted to drinking, eating, gambling, music and dancing girls, while the rooms on the second were reserved for private banquets, catered orgies, and smaller bedrooms where the house girls entertained special customers on a more individual basis. The fourth floor was for slaves of the third floor guests. Adjoining buildings, connected to the main building by colonnades, contained more lodgings and more rooms for the house women to entertain customers.

After washing up and resting, Vulso went to the judge's room. Alexander was already there. All three men had dressed for the evening. Vulso had changed from his military uniform into a dark red tunic with yellow *clavi* and a wide leather belt. Alexander had on an orange-yellow tunic with black *clavi* and a black belt, while Severus was putting on a purple tunic with white *clavi* and a narrow white belt. They all looked sharp and stylish.

"The oil lamp in my room has a picture of Hercules having sex with two little cupids," said Vulso. "What does this one have?"

Severus looked at the oil lamp on the table by his bed. "It looks like Leda and the Swan enjoying each other."

They both turned to Alexander. "I didn't notice," he answered their looks.

Severus headed for the door. "Let's go downstairs and have some food, a few drinks and watch the dancing girls. Later," he rubbed his hands together, "the dice tables."

It was only the 10th hour of the day, still afternoon, but the Blue Oyster was already going full blast. It was noisy and lively. Severus and his aides took seats at a table in one of the two large halls on the first floor. They ordered wine and Lucanian sausages and couldn't keep from ogling the scantily clad slave-waitress who took their orders.

A troupe of six Spanish Dancing Girls were energetically dancing the rhythmic and obscene *cordax* to the clicking of their castanets and the accompaniment of a twenty-man orchestra of lyres, flutes, drums and tambourines. It was both rousing and arousing, as intended.

"I have nothing against your villa," said Vulso as he watched the dancers, "but this is really much better." He spoke a little loudly to overcome the noise of the music and the crowd.

The dance ended in a frenzied burst of gyrations by the dancers, a loud and rapid crescendo from the orchestra and enthusiastic cheers and applause from the audience.

"When do you think Artemisia will arrive?" asked Vulso, as he picked up a piece of sausage with his fingers and began to eat.

"Late tonight," answered the judge. "I had one of our Imperial Post messengers take a message to her. When she hears we're going to spend the night at the Blue Oyster, she'll come as fast as she can."

The orchestra struck up a stately song in the martial Dorian mode and two other girls ran on stage, singing a song about a soldier who dressed up as one of the gods to seduce a shy, young farm girl. The lyrics were funny and obscene.

Alexander nodded at the girls. "They look enough alike to be sisters. I wonder if they're the Syrians that Cyclops was sleeping with."

"They're not bad looking either," observed Vulso smiling. "Cyclops may have died happily."

Severus thought for a moment and then smiled. He turned to his police aide. "How would you like to question them, Vulso? I know how industrious you can be when we're on a case. Perhaps you would like to start the investigation late tonight?"

Vulso grinned broadly and signalled the slave waitress. "I'll ask if they're available tonight and how much they cost. The government is paying, I presume. They may be expensive."

"Of course," replied the judge. "We're on an expense account while the investigation is under way and if the government sends us to Baiae, it'll have to pay for it."

They finished their drinks and snacks and Severus and Vulso headed into the gambling hall. Alexander begged off. "I'm not interested in gambling, so I'll go to my room and read."

The gambling room was large and filled with the sounds of dice rattling and men and women cheering and groaning. The walls were frescoed with gambling scenes. Ten burly men who looked like gladiators or wrestlers were stationed against the walls all around the hall. They eyed everyone suspiciously, prepared to bounce anyone who got into a fight — a not infrequent occurrence in a Roman gambling hall. Many of the dice players gambled in pairs, sitting on stools opposite each other with a board resting on their laps. Others gambled around large tables. The house provided every game the customers might want. They ran an "odd and even" table, where the players guessed at concealed pebbles, shells and nuts, and backed their guesses with money. You could even play *micatio* against the house, where both players simultaneously raised a certain number of fingers on their right hand, and then each one tried to be the first to shout out the total number of fingers extended by both. The house player was so good from long experience, however, that few dared to play against him. Besides, unlike the proverbial expression for trustworthiness — "you could play *micatio* with him in the dark" — this particular house player looked untrustworthy even in broadest daylight.

But of all the gambling games, dice was the favorite and the favorite version was the simplest. Two or more players each rolled three dice out of a dice cup and whoever threw the highest number won. Everyone fervently prayed he would throw 'Venus' — three sixes, and that his opponents would throw 'Dog' — three ones.

Neither Severus nor Vulso threw Venus, but they both came close. The dice were working for them and they weren't loaded. Unfortunately, they didn't play at the high-stakes tables, but they were content with winning a few hundred sesterces apiece.

Artemisia arrived at about the fourth night hour and joined them in the gambling hall. She was dressed stunningly in a pale blue v-necked sleeveless Greek dress, with a yellow waistband, a blue faience Egyptian necklace, a gold bracelet encrusted with turquoise stones and white shoes trimmed with gold. Her dark hair fell loosely below her shoulders. Her eyes gleamed.

There were many beautiful and fashionable women and men gambling, eyeing each other as well as the gaming boards and tables. Amid the noise and clamor of the hall, the shrieks of winners and the groans of losers, Artemisia now and then attracted her share of not-so-furtive looks from by both men and women. But none were more adoring or lustful than her husband's.

She first won a little, then lost a little, and then on her last throw, tossed Venus, beating out six other players at once. She walked away with more than 1,000 sesterces. It was a glorious evening.

Afterwards Marcus and Artemisia went to their room and made love, first lustfully, then passionately, and then lovingly. The orgasmic sounds from the orgy rooms below and from almost every other private room on their floor and the floor above were unneeded but inevitable stimulants to their own pleasure. No one got much sleep.

VI

VIBIA TELLS ABOUT CYCLOPS

The next morning at the third hour, Severus and Alexander boarded their Imperial Post carriage to take them from the Blue Oyster Inn to the Baiae villa of the Procurator T. Vibius Galba. Severus had sent a message the night before that he wanted to speak with the procurator's daughter Vibia, the reputed mistress of General Cyclops, and requested that she be home to receive him at that time.

"You're looking particularly calm and composed this morning,"observed Severus as they settled into their seats in the coach. "Almost serene."

"I am serene," replied Alexander, "and I have you to thank for it."

"Me, why?"

"For bringing me to this inn, this emporium of degradation and corruption."

Severus stared at him.

"You see," continued Alexander, "Here I was able to put my philosophy to a real test. I was able to exercise 'avoidance', as Epictetus advises, to discipline myself to avert desire and strive to obtain peace of mind, *tranquilitas*. Being tranquil in a country villa is one thing; being tranquil in that den of temptation is another."

"I not only admire you for it, Alexander, I envy you."

When they arrived, slaves helped the judge descend from the coach, making sure the hem of his toga did not touch the ground. An older slave ruefully apologized that the procurator was out hunting and his daughter Vibia was at the beach.

"Perhaps we're early," said the judge tactfully.

Alexander walked to an open area and held a palm sized sundial toward the sun. "It's hard to tell," he reported accurately.

"She's always late for everything and everyone," said the slave truthfully, and sent another slave running as fast as possible to fetch Vibia.

Vibia came back to the villa at a leisurely pace with a towel wrapped around her and an elegant looking young man with gold dust sprinkled on his hair clinging to her almost as closely as the towel. Severus didn't blame him. Vibia was very sexy.

After making the judge wait awhile longer until she changed, she eventually received him in the villa's library, reclining on a white cushioned couch. The tunic she had changed into was of sheerest Chinese silk and clung provocatively to her body. Severus sat in a comfortable chair in front of the couch, while Alexander sat in another chair, a stylus in one hand and a multi-leaved wax tablet in the other. He would be taking notes of the interview in Tironian shorthand.

"You're much younger than Judge Herminius," Vibia said to Severus, "and much better looking too."

"I'm here to talk about General Cyclops,"

Vibia frowned.

"You told Judge Herminius," he began directly, "that you didn't spend nights with the general, when in fact you did. Why did you lie to him?"

She giggled. "I also like your approach better than Herminius'. It's much more direct and forceful. Herminius is so stodgy."

"Look," said Severus with some agitation, "if you prefer to do this in a courtroom under oath with a stenographer taking down your words for the record, I can accommodate you."

"All right," she responded petulantly. "So I slept with Cyclops and I didn't tell that other judge. If the legal authorities are going to keep pestering me about it, I'll admit it and end the matter. I slept with him."

"How did you feel about Cyclops. Were you in love with him?"

She giggled again. "Judge! Just because he was a general doesn't mean I was in love with him. I may be only 19, but I'm not from the provinces. He was a refreshing change from boys my own age, though you understand I have nothing against them. But Cyclops was a general. I liked sleeping with him. And besides, he was cute. I never left his bed without giving him a little bite on his neck. It's too bad he didn't wait until after my vacation was over to kill Cyclops."

Severus was not sure he heard her correctly. "What do you mean by that? Who is 'he'? Do you know who killed the general?" He asked it incredulously.

"I don't," replied Vibia, "but Cyclops did. That is, he knew someone was going to try to kill him. He told me so."

"What did he tell you?"

"He used to brood about it. It was very exciting. It was almost like sleeping with a gladiator before he goes into the arena."

"I wouldn't know," said Severus.

"I would," countered Vibia.

"What did Cyclops tell you?"

"Not much. He said only that he'd seen someone from his past. Someone who might try to kill him. 'My Odysseus', he called him. I asked him to tell me about it, but he wouldn't. I thought he was joking anyway, that he was hinting at such things only to arouse me."

"Where did he see this Odysseus? Did he describe him at all or say anything about him?"

"I don't know. I think he saw him here at the Crater, but he really didn't say."

"Didn't Cyclops take any precautions to protect himself? Why didn't he just leave Baiae, for instance."

"He said there was no place to hide and even if there were, he was a general and wasn't going into hiding. If he were to be killed, he said, Baiae was as good a place as any. No, he wasn't afraid. He might even have been looking forward to the excitement of a deadly encounter. He once said it would get him ready for his next command."

"Can you think of anything else that might be important?"

"No."

Severus got up to leave. Alexander stood up as well. "Why didn't you tell this to Judge Herminius?" he asked. "You must have realized its importance."

"I asked my father about it. He's a procurator in the Bureau of the Treasury, you know, and he told me I didn't have to say anything. He said Cyclops probably told his other girl friends the same thing and Judge Herminius would find out from them. My father didn't want me to get involved."

"Then why are you telling me?" countered Severus.

She gave him a sly smirk and stretched her body on the couch like a cat. "Just because my father tells me something, it doesn't mean I'm going to do it. I just didn't feel like telling Judge Herminius. But now that you're interested in the case, I don't mind at all getting involved."

Severus left as quickly as possible.

VII

MESSALINA TELLS ABOUT BASSIANUS, MEHERDATES, CYCLOPS AND A MAN WITH A LIMP

When Severus returned to the Blue Oyster, he found a message in his room from Artemisia saying that she and Vulso had gone shopping in Baiae with their gambling winnings and they would be back in time for lunch. The judge decided to occupy the time by taking a look at the fish pool where the *curiosi* agent, Bassianus, had been drowned.

A slave at the front door gave him directions. The judge followed a dirt path which wound around the back of the building through manicured box hedges to a garden with marble benches on either side of a large rectangular pond. Summer flowers graced the garden with their colors and aromas, while the customary large garden sculpture of an erect phallus theoretically stimulated growth and averted evil. Lily pads and lotuses floated on the water while goldfish swam serenely amid the white and yellow blossoms. The judge sat on a bench, pondering the scene for a few minutes, idly throwing pebbles into the pond. Then he went back to the inn and asked for the proprietress, Messalina.

She appeared momentarily. Messalina was a handsome woman. Her careful use of cosmetics couldn't hide that she was no longer young, but her face didn't look old as much as experienced and interesting, even sedate. She wore a flashy cherry red tunic with a bright green waistband and her name was redolent of sex. As every Roman knew, the Empress Messalina, wife of Emperor Claudius a hundred years before, was a notorious nymphomaniac. She had even challenged Rome's most accomplished prostitute to a contest of who could have sex with the most men in one day. That Messalina won.

Severus introduced himself and directly brought up the subject of Bassianus and his demise in the fish pond.

"You'll want to see his room," said Messalina, and led the judge upstairs to the room where Bassianus had stayed. "The garden and fish pond area," she explained on the way up, "is used by guests during the day, but is usually deserted at night.

"If you ask me," she said as she opened the door with a key, "I'm not surprised something like this happened to him. There was something creepy about him. He reminded me of an insect." Her appraisal of Bassianus had a knowing air about it.

"Why do you say that?" asked the judge.

"He never wanted a girl at night. He never spoke to anyone. He always played for low stakes at the dice tables and he was always looking around, even when he was playing dice. I thought he was probably a criminal or a police agent — probably both."

The room they entered was one of the smaller ones at the inn. There was nothing but a bed, a stool, a table with an oil lamp, a washbasin and water pitcher.

"Who occupied the rooms on either side?" asked the judge.

"Two athletes on their way to the Games in Neapolis were in the room on the left. They were here enjoying a brief fling before their contests. My girls liked them. One was a discus hurler and the other a wrestler. The room on the right was occupied by a traveling jewel seller."

"Meherdates?"

"That's right. How did you know his name?"

"It was in the police report," replied Severus. "What do you know about him?"

"Not much. He said he was a traveling jewelry merchant touring the Crater and its inns and villas, trying to sell jewels to rich vacationing Romans. Or so he claimed."

"Didn't you believe him?"

"I rarely believe anyone."

Severus pointed at Messalina's hands and arms, decked out with rings and bracelets. "Did you buy any of those from him?"

"No. I tried to get him to show me his collection once I heard he was a jewelry salesman." She waved her arm at the judge. "I like jewels. But he said he never carried more than one or two pieces with him. It was too risky. I don't blame him, either. You probably saw our sign downstairs, that we don't accept liability for any gold, silver or jewels the customers bring with them. He said he kept his merchandise in a safe-deposit repository. He promised to get them out for me, but he never did. I suppose it was because he left so suddenly. It's too bad. He said he specialized in ropes of pearls and rubies. I might have bought something from him if he had shown me."

"You talked to him. Was he a Persian?"

"He said he was from Emesa, in Syria."

"Did he speak Latin?"

"I don't know. He was from the East so I naturally spoke to him in Greek because I don't know Aramaic. He spoke Greek well too. As if he had been educated. Not just the common Greek – the *koine* — everyone speaks."

Severus switched the subject.

"Did you know General Cyclops?"

"The one-eyed general who was murdered? Yes, of course. He used to come to the Blue Oyster almost every night. He loved to gamble and was interested in my Syrian dancing girls. But I never said much more than *salve* and *vale* to him."

"Did you ever see Meherdates talking to him? Perhaps trying to sell him jewelry?"

"No. I don't know if they knew one another, although it's possible. But I do remember times when they were both in the same hall at the same time, drinking or gambling or watching the entertainment but I don't remember ever seeing them together. I'll ask some of the slaves and other employees, if you'd like. They keep a sharp eye on things."

Severus nodded his head toward her in a positive gesture.

Messalina hesitated and thought for a moment. "It's funny that you should mention General Cyclops though. I wasn't the only one — even some of the bouncers in the dice hall noticed it — but Cyclops and this Bassianus used to watch each other. They always did it furtively, when the other wasn't looking. If you ask me, Cyclops and Bassianus were on to each other in some way." She mulled it over. "Do you think Meherdates killed both Bassianus and Cyclops? Is that what you're suggesting? I'm told he left the inn in a hurry, shortly after Cyclops was found dead on the beach and shortly before Bassianus was found dead in the pool. It is suspicious, isn't it?"

The judge didn't answer the question. He asked one instead.

"What kind of gambler was Cyclops?"

"The best one, from my point of view." She laughed. "He was a heavy loser and he kept coming back."

"I've been told he was here the night before he was killed? Did he win a lot that night?"

"I don't remember it personally, but after he was killed he was naturally the center of gossip for a few days. And everyone thought it was odd."

"What was?"

"Well, whenever he came here, he always gambled, at least for a little while. But that night — and Gorgo, one of my bouncers, commented on it — Gorgo said that Cyclops came here as usual in the evening, but didn't play at all. He looked very grim and just went back and forth from the gambling hall to the dance hall, between the inside of the inn and the outside, as if looking for someone. Gorgo saw him as he was leaving and chided him about only coming to look for women and not visiting the gambling tables."

"Did Cyclops say anything to that?"

"Yes. He gave Gorgo a big smile and said something like he had already won enough tonight."

"So he entered grimly and left smiling. Did he spend any time in the garden in back when he was looking around?"

"Gorgo thinks he did, but no one was actually watching him. Are you suggesting that it was General Cyclops who killed Bassianus? Because some of us gossiped about that the next day, and…."

That was exactly what Severus was thinking, but again he asked another question instead of replying. "Is there anything else you can tell me about Cyclops?"

"Yes, now that you mention it. It wasn't only this Bassianus that was exchanging looks with Cyclops. There was someone else as well. I don't know who he was. He didn't stay at the Blue Oyster and none of my staff recognized him. I know because we all talked about it later on. But one time this man and Cyclops were in the gambling hall and it was noticed – they kept staring at each other. Cyclops knew him and he knew Cyclops. And the looks they exchanged weren't furtive, like Cyclops and Bassianus. No, these were looks of hatred. It was daggers they were staring at each other; there was murder in their eyes."

"What did he look like?"

"He was about the same age as Cyclops, and he was big and strong. He looked like he might have once been a soldier, but he walked with a walking stick and a pronounced limp."

Severus and Alexander were having lunch when Artemisia and Vulso returned from their shopping trip.

Artemisia showed him an amethyst bracelet with gold filigree work. "I found it in an antique store," she said. "It's lovely, isn't it? I also bought two new pairs of shoes and a silk *palla* at a very expensive Baiae shop. I'll try it on for you tonight." She then displayed presents for the children. "I bought Flavia a new three-leaved wax tablet and a stylus, perfect to write her poems on and for Aulus, look at this." She handed her husband a small tear drop shaped piece of amber. "Look at it closely."

"There's a bee in it," he exclaimed. "How interesting." He studied it more closely. "You can see all the details of the bee. Aulus will love it."

"And for our smallest 'chick', I got Quintus his own set of wooden letter blocks for learning how to read."

A slave-waitress came to the table to take Artemisia and Vulso's orders for lunch. Severus recommended the oysters with the cumin, vinegar and honey dressing that he was having. Alexander was eating a plain grilled fish.

Artemisia tasted one of her husband's oysters. "It has some mint in the dressing too. Very tasty. But Alexander's grilled fish looks better. Is it fresh?" Alexander nodded 'yes' and the waitress added, "Caught this morning, *domina*. And we have a nice Alexandrian sauce for it."

"I'll have that, but I want the sauce on the side, not poured over the fish. And I would like asparagus with it."

Vulso, an oyster lover, ordered the dish Severus was having, but with twice as many oysters.

"So, Vulso," said Severus, "did you learn anything last night from the Syrian girls?"

Vulso returned a smile. "I learned a lot — even something about General Cyclops."

"What?"

"It's interesting. Cyclops thought someone was going to kill him. Cyclops called him 'my Odysseus'."

"I heard the same thing from Vibia," said Severus. "What did the girls say?"

"Just that. He made remarks about how he was going to spend his last days in drinking, gambling and sex. One of the sisters told him to stop joking, he was in perfect health. But Cyclops said he wasn't joking, someone was going to kill him. The girls still thought it was one of his jokes until they learned he had been murdered."

"What about the night he was killed. He was here at the Blue Oyster. Did he spend any time with them?"

"One of the sisters, the younger one, said she saw him here. He was looking for someone. She thought it was her, but he brushed her off. He didn't even take his cloak off, she said. She never saw him again. Everything else I learned doesn't concern the case. But I can tell you this. Cyclops had a good time during his last days."

Lunch for Vulso and Artemisia arrived and Severus told them about his interviews with Vibia and Messalina while they ate.

"So," asked Artemisia, "do you think Cyclops killed Bassianus and then this 'Odysseus' killed Cyclops? Or did Odysseus kill them both? And who is the man with the limp?"

Severus shrugged.

"What are you going to do now?" she asked. "Are we going to stay here and look for the man with the limp and get to go gambling again tonight?"

"I think we should go back to the villa this afternoon. Flaccus, Straton and Proculus should be there by now and I have something for us to do tomorrow. I'll ask

Judge Herminius to have the local *Vigiles* scour the area for any man with a limp."

"Vulso," the judge turned to his aide, "you're going back to Rome. I want you to investigate Cyclops' past. Get his army records. There's a complete dossier on every soldier, isn't there? From recruitment to retirement?" Vulso nodded in agreement. "See what's in Cyclops' file. Something in his past — someone he called 'Odysseus' — seems to have caught up with him. I want to know what or who it is. Talk to some of your contacts in the army. They might know things about Cyclops that aren't in the records. And see what 'smoke' the *curiosi* have on him. They were interested in Cyclops and must have their own file. There should be reports from their agents, probably even from Bassianus.

"And also find out more about Bassianus' assignment to follow Cyclops. How long has it been going on? If Cyclops killed him, why then and not some earlier time? Why at all? What was his motive? And why would he kill Bassianus on the same night he himself was murdered?" They got up from the table.

"What are you going to do while I'm in Rome?" asked Vulso. "Look for Meherdates?"

"To be more precise, Vulso, I'm also going to look for Meherdates and Meherdates' jewels."

SCROLL III

VIII

VULSO GOES TO *CURIOSI* HEADQUARTERS

*C*uriosi headquarters were located in the Castra Peregrina — 'the Camp of the Wanderers' — in Rome's fashionable *regio* II, the Caelian Hill region, not far from the luxury apartment house where Severus lived. The four long porticoed buildings which served as *curiosi* barracks and administrative offices were among the few public buildings in an area filled with aristocratic mansions and expensive apartment houses, as well as high class inns, taverns and brothels.

The imperial secret service specialized in political and military intelligence, internal security, domestic and foreign spying and any other delicate or confidential jobs the government had in mind. They were directly responsible to the emperor or, in his place, the Prefect of Praetorians, and were headed by the Princeps of the Wanderers.

Vulso, an army veteran, knew all about their beginnings, for they originated in the supply section of the legions. They were still, in fact, known officially as *fru-mentarii* — grain dealers. In legions scattered in camps across the Empire, outside cities or on the frontiers, it was the soldiers responsible for buying food, especially grain, who because they frequently visited the local markets had the most contact with the local population. These contacts enabled them to observe conditions and almost routinely pick up information about what was happening in their areas. The legions soon began to rely on them for intelligence to gauge the mood of the local population or learn from merchants and travelers about happenings across the borders.

Vulso also knew that about 75 years before, in the reign of Domitian, someone had the idea of pooling their knowledge and making it available to the government in Rome by detaching *frumentarii* from each legion and bringing them to Rome for temporary duty. This way, the planners in the capital could get an overview of what was happening and move troops to anticipate or meet threats. The constant coming and going of *frumentarii* between Rome and the provinces earned them the nickname "wanderers".

A great advance in their functions occurred during the reign of Hadrian, the predecessor of Antoninus Pius. Hadrian had spent much of his reign touring the empire in a conscientious effort to personally bring good government to the provinces. But his absences from Rome meant that someone had to keep a close eye on developments in the capital and particularly make sure that no one would try to take advantage of his absence to dethrone him. The *frumentarii*, experienced in gathering military intelligence and in undercover work in the provinces, easily adapted themselves to collecting political intelligence in the capital as well. And their industry in prying soon won them the sobriquet "*curiosi*".

The story was still told of one of their early successes under Hadrian. It seems that the wife of one of Hadrian's courtiers wrote her husband a letter complaining he was so preoccupied with pleasures and the baths that he never came home. *Curiosi* agents secretly read the letter and reported it to the emperor. Sometime later, when the courtier asked Hadrian for a vacation from court, the emperor reproached him with his fondness for his baths and his pleasures. "What!" exclaimed the surprised courtier, "did my wife write you just what she wrote me?"

Their political intelligence function once acquired, the *curiosi* began to expand their activities. From simply following people about, eavesdropping on conversations or trying to read their letters, the *curiosi* thoroughly infiltrated the Imperial Post and read mail at will. They secretly opened their own inns on the roads to eavesdrop on foreigners and travelers and were beginning to move into other areas by taking over prisons and forced labor camps. Agents even attended theater performances and supervised mime spectacles to watch for anti-government expressions. A notorious trick practiced by *curiosi* agents was to dress in civilian clothes, sit down next to someone on a bench in some public place, and begin to speak ill of the emperor. If the unsuspecting victim agreed, he could be arrested. Fortunately, most people had only good things to say about Marcus Aurelius.

Although anyone subversive was of interest to the *curiosi*, they concentrated their attentions on senators, generals and other people of influence in and out of the government. They also kept an eye on particularly sub-versive groups like the Christians, whose refusal to offer wine and incense to statues of the emperor or the state gods was notorious and considered subversive and dan-gerously unpatriotic.

And now, Vulso had heard, the *curiosi* were acquir-ing even another nickname in the provinces. For the Bureau of the Treasury was quick to appreciate their co-ercive talents and beginning to employ them to enforce the collection of taxes. The Greeks were now referring to them as *kollectiones* — revenuers.

Vulso was received politely at *curiosi* headquarters. He didn't get to see the Princeps, few people did, but he was received by a centurion, a liaison between the impe-rial secret service and the City's police forces. The centu-rion introduced Vulso to a *curiosi* agent named Brennus, who had Cyclops' file. They sat on stools around a low table.

Brennus had blond hair and blue eyes, sunken cheeks and a thin mouth. He looked clever. His name was a latin-ized form of a name from Gaul or Britannia, but his Latin was pure city of Rome. He would naturally be someone from the lower classes, with the status of *humilior* under the law, since the *curiosi*, who mostly investigated sen-ators and equestrians, were reluctant to employ agents with their legal status of *honestior*. Brennus knew all about General Cyclops.

"If it's 'smoke' you want," he told Vulso as he opened the file, "I'll give you 'smoke'.

"Cyclops' original name was Gnaeus Avidianus Nepos. He was born in the third year of the reign of

Trajan." Brennus took a moment to figure it out. "That would make him 61 when he was killed. He was from the province of Illyria, the son of a shopkeeper — a spice dealer. His grandfather was a slave.

"At the age of 19 Nepos enlisted in the army and was assigned to the Legion VIII Augusta on the Rhine frontier in Germania. That year there was a revolt in Britannia and he was part of a detachment sent from his legion to reinforce Legion XX Valeria Victrix. That's where he lost his eye and won a field commission. As a reward for his bravery, he was made a centurion on the spot. Evidently proud of his wound, he officially added the name Cyclops to his cognomen.

"Cyclops was then assigned to various legions throughout the Empire, but saw no action for the next thirteen years. When the revolt in Judaea broke out in the 15th year of Hadrian's reign — 30 years ago — Cyclops was with the Legion XXII Deiotariana based in Egypt."

"Wasn't that the legion that was disbanded in disgrace?" asked Vulso.

"Yes. They were so lax from easy living and not fighting that they performed miserably. Sounds familiar, doesn't it," commented Brennus wryly in obvious allusion to the current problem with the eastern legions in the war with Persia. "In any event, you may remember the scandal. In engagements with the Judaeans, the XXIInd were cut to pieces. One whole cohort was so careless that they were wiped out in their own mess hall by poisoned wine that the Jews had contrived to feed them.

"Because of the failure of the XXII Deiotariana, troops from all over the Empire had to be brought in to quell the revolt. There were at least four full legions and detachments from five others. Hadrian even had to go there in person. The XXII was disbanded and struck from the rolls, its men carrying the stigma ever afterwards."

"What happened to Cyclops?"

"Somehow he survived it." Brennus looked through his documents. "It's a little strange, actually. He was court-martialed for desertion at one point, but was acquitted. Then the next thing I have from the records is that he was raised to the Equestrian Class, promoted to tribune and transferred out of the war zone. In fact, it says here, he was put in command of a cohort of auxiliaries — The First Cohort of Thebans — and was sent to fight barbarians in Germania."

"How did that happen?" asked Vulso, perplexed. "For instance, where did he get the 400,000 sesterces to qualify for the Equestrian Class?"

"I don't know," answered Brennus, also perplexed. "Perhaps he had connections. Maybe a patron. I don't know."

"But let me finish his file for you. For about ten years Cyclops served in various posts in Germania and then spent five years fighting Berbers on the frontier in Africa. He was finally raised to the rank of legate, a general, and as all legates must be, he became a member of the Senatorial Class." Brennus scratched his head and looked up at Vulso. "I don't know where he got the million sesterces to qualify for the Senatorial Class, but evidently he had it. Anyway, for a short time he was in command of the Legion XII Fulminata on the Euphrates frontier with Persia and then he was brought to army headquarters in Rome as a military advisor. That's where he got into trouble with the government because of his opposition, in fact his notorious outspoken opposition, to the Emperor Antoninus' peace policy. He was in Baiae on, shall we say, inactive service. He had been told to take a long furlough, though of course in view of the current Persian invasion he was about to be recalled to duty."

Brennus looked directly at Vulso. "That's one reason we must find out who killed him. We're at war. Cyclops was to be given an important command in the war. So this may be an assassination, a stroke of the *spasaka* – the Persian secret service. We have to know if they're behind it."

Vulso nodded understandingly. "So far the only Persian connection we've come across is that a jeweler with a Persian name – Meherdates – visited the general on the afternoon before he was murdered, had an argument with him, and was thrown out of Cyclops' villa. We're trying to track him down. But would a Persian spy use a Persian name?"

"I don't know. Persians are subtle and tricky. Just keep trying to find him. We'll supply more men if you need them."

Vulso then returned to the subject of Cyclops himself. "What sort of a commander was Cyclops?"

"A strict disciplinarian. His men generally hated him. You know the type. He made his men drink vinegar instead of wine. But he was a man of action, personally brave and daring. He liked to be in the thick of the fight himself and had the medals to prove it. He won the Gold Crown, the Silver Spearshaft and the Silver Standard. When he became a general, of course, he acquired a lot more, but that was only for being a general."

"Forget about the medals," interrupted Vulso. "I want to know how he first got the 400,000 sesterces to become an Equestrian."

"From booty?" suggested Brennus lamely.

"From booty?" replied Vulso incredulously. "Centurions don't get that kind of booty. If they did, I would probably be sitting in the Senate myself. Besides, booty comes from victory and Cyclops' legion was disastrously defeated."

Vulso thought a moment. "Do you have any other information about that period in his life? What about the court-martial for desertion. What was that all about? It happened just before his promotion, didn't it?"

"Yes. Let me look through the file again. I think I have...Yes, here it is. I have a clerk's extract of the trial." He handed it to Vulso. "But he was acquitted, as I said."

Vulso took the papyrus document and read it.

"Year 15 of Hadrian, in the Consulship of Pontianus and Rufinus.

Gnaeus Avidianus Nepos Cyclops, centurion of Legion XXII Deiotariana, had been accused of desertion on the Kalends of December and for three days thereafter, along with the soldiers Herculanus, Gaianus and Candidus.

The centurion Cyclops declared that he had taken a squad to guard the Temple of Atargatis in the district of Caesarea; that thereafter the squad was ambushed by rebels and the temple sacked. Cyclops further stated that the soldiers Herculanus, Gaianus and Candidus were killed and he was taken captive, but that thereafter Cyclops escaped.

T. Vibius Galba then discussed it with his assessor and declared:

The centurion Cyclops was guarding a temple, was made captive, and escaped."

Vulso finished reading and laughed out loud. "That explains the money. Cyclops robbed the temple!"

"How can you know that?" countered Brennus. "The judge heard the evidence and acquitted him."

"That's just it," replied Vulso. "The judge at Cyclops' court martial was T. Vibius Galba. Do you know who he is?"

"No."

"This same Galba is presently vacationing in Baiae and has the villa next to Cyclops'. Also his daughter Vibia was Cyclops' mistress."

"By Hercules!" exclaimed Brennus. "That's not in the files. Why didn't that idiot Bassianus find out about this? What do you think it means, centurion?"

"I'm not sure. But do me a favor and see what you have on this Galba. He's a procurator with the Bureau of the Treasury."

"I'll check, but it might take a few days."

"And speaking of Bassianus, Judge Severus told me to tell you that he strongly suspects your agent was killed by Cyclops. But why the general turned on him is not known. So, among other things, the judge wants to know when Bassianus started following Cyclops."

Brennus looked through the file for a bit. "O yes, here it is. Cyclops has been a subject of interest, shall we say, for quite a while. Naturally there were a number of different agents over that time, but Bassianus took over the assignment of following him two days before the Ides of July, so it was almost three weeks before Bassianus was killed."

Vulso stood up. "Now I'm going to try to find if the records of the XXII Deiotariana might be here in Rome, perhaps in one of the Tabularia buildings. I'll check at the office of the Urban Quaestor. He's in charge of the state archives."

"The records may be in Egypt, where the XXIInd was based," suggested Brennus.

"Yes, but there may be copies in Rome. There must have been a board of inquiry, maybe even a Senate investigation, that investigated the performance of the XXIInd, and those records should be in Rome. Maybe I can find a complete transcript of the court martial trial. I would like to know more than what's contained in the extract."

"We got the extract from Cyclops' army records," said Brennus, "but there wasn't a trial transcript included."

"There wouldn't be," answered Vulso. "The extract is sufficient for army use."

Vulso got up to leave. "If you come up with anything on Galba, send it by messenger to Judge Severus' chambers in the Forum of Augustus. I'm going to the State Record Office and search through the archives."

Vulso and ten court slaves spent three days in the Tabularium in the Old Forum, amid the huge stone vaults on a basement level. There they waded through dusty baskets, boxes and chests filled with ledgers, papyrus scrolls and bronze record tablets. They sifted through personnel files, roster sheets, legionary payroll accounts, legionary bank records, honorable discharge certificates, ignominious discharge certificates, procurement files, military diplomas, requests for transfer forms, birth declarations, recruitment papers and all the other numerous documents and files connected with legionary administration.

They also found some of the various court martial proceedings and board of inquiry reports that arose out of the disbanding of the XXII Deiotariana, but it was here that difficulties arose. It was clear that others had been at the files before Vulso. There were occasional mysterious notations among the documents that files had been removed "for official investigation", but many of these notations were undated and illegibly recorded the names of those who had taken the files out. There were even occasional mutilations and inking out of names or important sections of court records. In fact, the records of the XXII Deiotariana were a mess. A lot of money must have been spent to get at those records, but then, thought Vulso, a lot of reputations must have been involved to make it worthwhile.

At the end of three days searching, Vulso was convinced that the transcript of Cyclops' court-martial wasn't there. Perhaps it never had been. But one of the court slaves found something else of interest — duty rosters for Candidus, Gaianus and Herculanus, the soldiers of Cyclops' doomed patrol.

From his army experience Vulso realized that duty rosters had something to tell. In a peacetime army the ordinary soldier doesn't always do strictly military chores. There aren't enough of them and it's a waste of manpower. Instead they get special assignments from time to

time. When Vulso was with the Legion II Traiana Fortis
in Egypt, soldiers were always being assigned to papyrus manufacture. Others got dredging duty to keep the
harbors clean, others were assigned to the granary or to
work in legionary brick kilns. There were hundreds of
such jobs and soldiers could have these assignments for
months at a time before returning for periods of patrols
or maneuvers. They go back and forth and acquire a certain expertise in these jobs. With this in mind, the nature of the specialties of Cyclops' patrol members struck
Vulso as provocative. Candidus had been in the legion's
clerical and documents section; Herculanus' special duties were with the army's vehicles and transport, while
Gaianus had been assigned to the mint in Alexandria.

Vulso mulled that over. "Documents, transportation,
coinage," he said to himself. "Documents, transportation, coinage," he repeated to himself. Vulso started
to grin; then he started to laugh. Then a sardonic look
played over his face. "Cyclops and his patrol robbed that
temple." He looked at the duty rosters again. "And I can
now make a very good guess about how they got away
with it."

IX

JUDGE SEVERUS INVESTIGATES IN PUTEOLI

While Vulso was in Rome conferring with the *curiosi* and searching the state archives, Judge Severus spent a few days at his villa in Neapolis reading, swimming, sleeping and just generally relaxing until his aides, Flaccus, Straton and Proculus, arrived from Rome.

Gaius Sempronius Flaccus was the judge's judicial assessor. He was young and a recent graduate from the law school of Sabinus and Cassius in Rome, the same school Severus and his father and grandfather had attended. The assessor's job was to aid the judge, especially to sit with the judge on the Tribunal and help him reach decisions on the cases before the court. Flaccus had Equestrian status and was a good young lawyer whose opinion Severus valued. He was also smart and full of wisecracks. His ambition, he had once told the judge, was to make a lot of money and become a prefect.

Publius Aelianus Straton was, like Vulso, a member of the Urban Cohort in Rome, but his rank, *tesserarius*, below that of centurion. Straton was a Greek by birth and had been raised in childhood as a slave in the imperial household of Emperor Publius Aelius Hadrianus. He had been manumitted on Hadrian's death, and as a freed slave of a Roman citizen had automatically become a Roman citizen himself. But Straton was still embittered by his experiences as a slave and was often violently anti-Roman in his opinions. Nevertheless, he was personally loyal to the judge and he was a capable investigator, even a talented one. Lean, short and ordinary looking, with sad brown eyes, he could pass almost anywhere as anyone, from a wandering philosopher to a carriage driver, from a slave to a member of the imperial household.

Quintus Proculus, Severus' court clerk, was sixty-years-old and had spent his life in the law courts. He knew more about the practice of law than most lawyers and judges. When the tribunal was in session, Proculus was the court reporter, recording all proceedings in Tironian Notes shorthand. He was also in charge of the court's clerical and administrative functions and oversaw the squads of court slaves in their duties. He loved details and so no detail escaped his eyes. "Do you have to notice everything?" was often a question posed to him testily from someone he caught in a very small slip-up. Proculus also loved Roman law and the Roman courts and did all he could to enhance the competence, dignity and prestige of both. Severus regarded him as rather straight-laced and prudish, but knew he was invaluable and that the court couldn't function properly without him.

Each evening messengers arrived from the police stations in various towns on the Crater informing the judge of the progress, or lack of it, in the search for Meherdates or his jewels. The inns in all the smaller towns had been canvassed quickly and without success and the search was now focusing in and around the city of Puteoli, the commercial-industrial center and largest port at the Crater, situated between Baiae and Neapolis. The size and international character of the city made it a likely place for an oriental to lose himself and the busy port gave access to passenger ships and foreign travel. But a check of the city's inns and hotels had turned up nothing and Meherdates' name didn't appear on any ship manifest, either departing or arriving. Aramaic speaking agents had been sent into the oriental sections of Puteoli to ask questions and keep their eyes and ears open, and local police informers were pressed for information. But neither tactic resulted in even one iota of information about Meherdates.

In the last few days, the police had concentrated on making the rounds of all safe-deposit repositories in the city. They checked all banks, all privately owned repositories and all government safe-deposit buildings, showing copies of the painting of Meherdates to the custodians and attendants.

On the fifth day of the search, someone was found who recognized the picture. It was the custodian of a government owned repository near the harbor in Puteoli, in the section of the city rented by the Lebanese city of Tyre as a trading concession. The man in the picture, the custodian had told the police officers, had appeared at the repository five days before the Kalends of August and again one day after the Kalends. The day after the Kalends, Severus recalled, was also the day Meherdates left the Blue Oyster Inn and the day after General Cyclops was killed.

Early the next morning, Judge Severus and his police aide Straton took their imperial post carriage to Puteoli. There they were met by a local policeman and trans-ferred to sedan-chairs, since Puteoli, like Rome, tried to control its excessive traffic by banning wheeled vehicles and horses on the streets during the day.

They found the repository in the lower town, near the harbor, on a busy commercial street lined with small shops and decaying four-story apartment houses, in an area which appeared once to have been thriving. The police officer, Floranus, bemoaned Puteoli's decline, explaining that the Emperor Trajan's modernization of the port of Ostia, close to Rome, had captured much of Puteoli's commerce, including the valuable Egyptian grain trade. He swept his arm to indicate the street scene and said that there were other trading stations in Puteoli owned by other cities and peoples, but that this one, the Tyrian section, was superior in adornment and size to all the others. Once, Floranus said, it had been more numer-ous and wealthy, but now the residents were constantly complaining that the upkeep of their temples and their community and the 400,000 sesterces yearly rent for the trading concessions was too costly. Business wasn't so good anymore and without subsidies from the city of Tyre they could not manage.

Arriving at the repository building, Judge Severus descended from his litter while the police officer made sure the reddish-purple bordered hem of his judicial toga didn't touch the ground. The judge stopped in front of the entrance and read the placard, announcing in the usual terms the services and rules of the repository:

"In these repositories of the Emperors Marcus Aurelius and Lucius Verus are for hire grain space, lock-up space, close storage safes, column-safes and space for safes with service of custodians from today and the Kalends of January.

"Rules of the repository: Anyone wishing to retain for a further year the safe or whatever else he rents must have paid up and give notice before the Ides of December.

"No liability is undertaken for gold and silver.

"All property stored in these repositories will be sub-ject to a lien to the contractor against due payment of rent.

"If anyone renting space in these repositories leaves his property there without making it over under seal to the custodian, the contractor will not be liable."

Inside, the judge was introduced to Petilius, the cus-todian, a round little man with a quick smile and voluble tongue. He appeared pleased by the opportunity to be the center of attention. Straton unrolled the painting of Meherdates and showed it to Petilius, who addressed his answers to the judge, using his Equestrian honorific title.

"Yes, that's the one, *eminentissime*. I remember him, as I told the *Vigiles* yesterday. We get a lot of orientals in here. We're in the middle of the Tyrian trading station, you know. He came in a few weeks ago with a priest..."

"A priest? Who..."

"Yes. I could tell from the way he was dressed. His tunic had symbols of a shovel, a thunderbolt, a laurel wreath and a *sistrum*, you know that musical rattle instrument. So I asked what it all was, and he said he was a priest of Mithra…"

"Mithra?" interjected Severus, "the Persian sun god?"

"That's right. He said he was a 'Lion', a priest of the 4th rank, and invited me to come to the Mithraeum sometime to learn about the mysteries of Mithra. He said his name was Suren and to ask for him at the Mithraeum. It's only a few streets away.

"Now, *eminentissime*, I don't hold with these foreign cults. The old Roman gods are good enough for me, and besides they have all those strange rites. You can see them all the time on the street. You know, eunuchs for priests, prostitutes for priestesses. They're always whipping themselves and holding sex orgies in their temple down the street, although that may be the cult of the Syrian fish-goddess, not Mithra worshipers. But really, *eminentissime*, I can't tell one from the other. Not that I've ever attended one of their sex orgies, but everyone knows what they do in there. Not that I have anything against sex rites, *eminentissime*, but..."

Severus tried to interject a question, but failed.

"...I can see that you're interested in the man. Well, as I said, he was with the Mithra priest Suren. Cultists come in here all the time. You should see the money and gold and jewels they collect. I guess they don't trust themselves to keep their hands off the valuables. That's why they often deposit them with me for safe keeping. But this priest wasn't the regular one that brings in the valuables from the temple..."

"What did they want?" Severus managed to ask.

"The priest asked for a safe-deposit box, of course. He had a package all wrapped up. Not too small, not too big." He held his hands about two feet apart. "I have the records."

Petilius went to a table and opened a ledger.

"My records say they came in five days before the Kalends of August and the safe is in the name of the Suren, the priest. The day after the Kalends they both returned, took the package out of the safe and into one of the private rooms, and then returned it to the safe."

"It's still here?"

"Yes. The rent is paid up until the Kalends of January. If you give me a court order I can open it for you."

"I will have one drawn up," answered Severus.

"In the meantime," interjected Straton, "you'll see that the *Vigiles* are notified if either the man or the priest returns to claim it."

Petilius nodded affirmatively.

Severus asked a question. "You said you have mostly orientals as customers. Why do you remember the one in the painting particularly?"

"I remember a lot of my customers. But the one you're interested in, the one with the priest, I remember because of the way he talked to me. Not that he did much talking. But I'm a friendly fellow and I like to talk to all my customers. You know, just to pass the time. So while the paper work was being done, I asked him where he was from. I like to find out where my customers are from. I learn about the world that way. I learn many strange and wondrous things about the East. They have peculiar customs there..."

"Yes. Your interest is commendable. What did he say?"

"Now you know orientals. Always chattering away. They always talk to me. I speak to them in Greek. I know a few words of Aramaic because they're my usual customers and I've picked up a few words, but I speak to them in Greek."

"What did he say?"

"That's what I'm getting to, *eminentissime*. The first time they were here I tried to make friendly conversation. But the man, the one in the painting, spoke to me in this high-class Greek, not in the common dialect everyone speaks, but like he was some aristocratic snob and I was some farm slave. I didn't like it much, I can tell you that. So the second time he was here, the day after the Kalends, I got even.

"They came in during the afternoon, after the siesta, and when I saw he was in a great hurry, I made like I couldn't find the right ledger or didn't know exactly where the box was — you know, just to annoy him. I made him wait quite a long time. By the time I was through, he was pacing up and down and cursing, and not in high-class Greek either." Petilius chuckled at the thought of it. "So I'm very happy to see he's in trouble with the law."

Judge Severus, Straton and Floranus left the repository intending to continue on to the Temple of Mithra, which the policeman said was only a few streets away. The morning was now well along, the streets were crowded and the sun was broiling. They stopped for a quick drink and a snack at a small tavern across the street from the repository, and stood on the sidewalk at the tavern's street stand drinking cold wine and munching honey buns.

"We should have come with a court order to open the safe," said Straton between bites.

"My jurisdiction in Baiae is questionable enough as it is, Straton," answered the judge. "Here, in Puteoli, I have none at all. I'll have to get one from a local judge. In fact, I'll have to have Flaccus research the law for me. I know there's no trouble in opening a safe-deposit box if the rent is overdue, but here the rent is paid up. Also, the property appears to belong to the priest Suren, not to Meherdates, and we have nothing on him. I'm not sure we're entitled to a court order at all in this situation."

Severus turned to the local policeman. "Floranus, do you know this Mithraeum? Have you had any run-ins with it in the past?"

"Not really, judge. All I know is that a Mithra Temple is unlike every other temple. Other temples are generally beautiful, with columned facades, rare marbles, rich decorations and statues of the god or goddess inside, just like Roman or Greek temples. But temples of Mithra are in the dark basements of buildings or in caves. I don't know why. Something to do with their cult, with their so-called Mysteries."

"One mystery seems to be why a sun god is kept in a dark basement," commented Severus wryly. "And if the sun god is in a basement, where do they worship their god of the underworld? On the roof?"

"I've also heard about Mithra and their celebrations in Rome," said Straton. "I'm sure you have too. Disgusting! They put an initiate in a pit covered by wooden boards with openings, and put a bull over the pit, and slit its throat, allowing the blood to spill all over the initiate below. Like the Christian baptism, only some say the Christians use human blood, some even say baby's blood."

"Straton, you don't really believe that about the Christians, do you?"

"Why not? Everyone says so. How do I know what they do at their secret meetings? Egyptians and Jews mutilate their penis, the Atargatis fish-god cult from Syria parade in public cutting themselves and whipping themselves until the blood flows. The Christians are an eastern superstition too, so why should I doubt the bloody stories about what they do in private?"

"I can't believe anyone kills babies in their ceremonies," replied the judge. "That's just *vituperatio*. Even the learned Cornelius Fronto, in his recent speech against the Christians, never claimed they killed babies. What they do, he said, is have love-feasts, incestuous banquets and drunken sex orgies. And he called them atheists because they don't believe in the gods."

"But they proclaim that they drink the blood and eat the flesh of their god," countered Straton. "What do they use for that?"

'I don't know. But I don't believe they drink human blood. More likely it's red wine, if they're drinking it."

"It's all degraded," said Straton, "I don't understand why people are so fascinated with blood. Romans lust to see it in the arena, Persians pour it over their heads in the Mithra cult, Syrians cut it from their arms in the Atargatis cult, and Christians drink it in their ceremonies."

"Our world is often degraded," replied the judge simply. "That's why our Stoic philosophers teach us to harden ourselves against it and our Epicurean philosophers teach us to detach ourselves from it."

They arrived at the Mithraeum, located in the basement of an apartment block. It was dark inside, though a few torches set in wall sconces enabled them to see the wall frescoes depicting the slaughter of bulls. The smell of spicy incense permeated the place.

A temple slave greeted them with a bow and then ran to get one of the priests when he saw the policemen and Severus' judicial toga and heard the judge's command. Without much delay, a priest appeared, clad in an elaborate robe covered with jewels and metal threads and decorated with a variety of symbols like a shepherd staff and a mitre. He introduced himself as Zabuttas, the Father of the temple. He bowed low before the judge.

"Can I serve you, *eminentissime*," he said to the judge in heavily accented Latin.

"I wish to speak to the priest Suren."

"Perhaps you have the wrong temple," suggested Zabuttas. "We have no priest named Suren here. Perhaps he is from some other temple. We are often confused with other eastern religions, like Atargatis and Cybele and Magna Mater, *eminentissime*. But Mithra is a Persian god, Cybele is from Asia Minor and Atargatis is from Syria, and only one of the Syrian gods. There is Hadad, for instance..."

"There is no confusion," answered Severus sharply. "I have good information that a priest of Mithra named

Suren, of the rank of Lion was in the area on or around the Kalends of August, only two weeks ago."

"It is perhaps possible, *eminentissime*, but if so, he is not a regular priest of this temple. We often have members of our cult staying here for short periods of time, usually waiting for a ship to depart or breaking a journey if they disembark at Puteoli. You see, our priests often engage in their own business and often stay at our temples while in transit. He may be one of them. But I have never heard of him, though I would be happy to inquire of members of our Mithraeum."

Severus nodded. "Do so. I will have a messenger check back with you tomorrow."

Severus nodded to Straton who produced the painting of Meherdates and showed it to the priest.

"Do you recognize this man?" asked the judge.

Zabuttas looked at the painting. "I have never seen him, *eminentissime*."

Severus told the priest that the name of the man in the picture was Meherdates and that he was a jewel merchant. "When you ask your priests about Suren, ask also about Meherdates."

Zabuttas bowed low. "*Eminentissime*," he said, "it is always a pleasure to cooperate with the authorities."

The judge and his aide then left the temple. "It is always a pleasure to cooperate with the authorities," mimicked Severus. "I can hardly wait."

Straton laughed. "These are Persians and we are at war with Persia. Do you think there are Persian spies here?"

"The *curiosi* suspect that the 'Eye' of the Great King – the *spasaka* — is everywhere. So why not here? Yes, Straton, why not here?"

Zabuttas watched them go until they were well outside the temple and out of sight. Then he ran to the back. "I want a slave messenger immediately," he yelled in his squeaky voice. "Immediately," he screamed.

X

THE PROCURATOR T. VIBIUS GALBA IS QUESTIONED IN COURT

"The most eminent Procurator Titus Vibius Galba," announced a court slave as he opened the door to Judge Severus' temporary chambers in the Baiae courthouse. A short, fat man strode briskly in, flashed a toothy grin, and exchanged a greeting kiss with Judge Severus. The judge caught a strong whiff of perfume as he invited the procurator to sit on the chair across from his own.

Four days had passed since Severus' trip to safe-deposit repository in Puteoli. During that time, a message from the Temple of Mithra alleged that a priest named Suren had stayed there for about a week. His native town was somewhere in Syria and he had left for Rome the day after the Kalends of August. Nothing else was known about him and no one had recognized the painting of Meherdates.

"Very informative," said the judge sarcastically.

Vulso had also returned from Rome with the information about Cyclops' court-martial and acquittal and his own theory of the temple robbery. He also had a brief background sketch of the Procurator Galba, provided by the *curiosi*.

Galba came from a family of slave traders who made a fortune selling male slaves to the arena and female slaves to brothels. And they used their money not only to buy Galba entry into the Equestrian Class, but to make sure everyone else forgot about his family background. The report also confirmed that Galba had been in Judaea at the time of the revolt. He had been on the staff of Tineius Rufus, the Procurator of Judaea, where he had been assigned to oversee the collection of provincial taxes. While the war was in progress, Galba was transferred to the staff of the Prefect of Syria in Antioch. He held a financial post there for five years and then went to Rome, where he held various jobs with the Bureau of the Treasury, rising to the rank of procurator three years ago.

"I assume you want to see me about my daughter," began Galba with a sweep of his hand that ostentatiously displayed expensive rings on each finger. Severus took an instant dislike to him. "If so," continued the procurator confidently, "I think you should consider that I'm a member of the Equestrian Class and a procurator in the Bureau of the Treasury. My department administers the farm-loan child welfare program for forty towns in Italy."

"I've heard of that program," commented the judge. "The Treasury makes loans to farmers to improve agriculture and gives the interest on the loans to local towns for the maintenance and education of poor children. It's a very worthy project."

"Yes," said Galba, "and I hold a Third Grade Procuratorship. That's 100,000 sesterces a year."

Galba paused to let the judge digest the title and salary and all they implied. "Now, he continued with a knowing smile, "is it really necessary to bother me or my daughter any longer?"

"That depends," answered Severus mildly. "Of course, I don't want to bother you or your daughter. I'm only interested in investigating the murder of General Cyclops. You knew him, didn't you?"

Galba hesitated. "Yes. That is, I met him."

Severus waited for the procurator to continue. Galba hesitated again, took an embroidered handkerchief from the folds of his toga and mopped his brow.

"He had the house next door. My daughter occasionally went boating with him."

"You knew him before that, though," suggested Severus.

"No...well, yes, as a matter of fact," he said casually. "I may have once met him in the East years ago." He mopped his brow again.

"When was that?"

"I'm not sure. A long time ago. How do you expect me to remember. I've met many people in my career."

Severus had by now decided not to mention the court-martial trial until Galba did. "So since that time in the East, you hadn't seen him until this summer?"

Galba surprised the judge with a show of anger. "What is this all about? First my daughter and now me. I don't have to take this. This is sheer harassment. I'm a Roman procurator. And you're from Rome, aren't you? Your message said you were a Judge in the Court of the

Urban Prefect in Rome. What's your jurisdiction here anyway? I don't have to answer your questions. We're not in a court in Rome."

Severus looked at him quizzically and answered him calmly. "I'm temporarily assigned to the court in Baiae, Procurator. You are of course welcome to inspect the authorizing documents. They're on file in the clerk's office in this building.

"Furthermore, I only asked you when you met General Cyclops. It's a simple question. Why are you so reticent? Are you hiding something?" Severus said it maliciously.

"I wish to consult a lawyer before I talk to you any further," answered Galba angrily. "I'm not accustomed to being questioned." He stood up. "You're not in court now, Judge Severus."

Severus remained seated and looked up at Galba. "I will be tomorrow. And so will you. You will be in my courtroom in this building tomorrow morning at the third hour. With or without your lawyer. And everything will be on the record."

"You'd better be well-connected," stormed the procurator as he turned to leave, "because if you're not, I'll break you. I'll end your career for treating me this way."

Galba walked out, slamming the door behind him.

Proculus entered, staring after Galba. "What happened? He looked livid."

"Galba is a fool," said Severus. "He tried to intimidate me. He even threatened me. So I ordered him into court tomorrow morning. If he tries the same thing there, I'll teach him a lesson he will never forget."

The next day, before the beginning of the court session, Judge Severus stopped by the chambers of Judge Herminius, ostensibly to thank him for making available his court's facilities. Actually, Severus was hoping to convince Herminius to sit with him on the Tribunal that morning to undercut any jurisdictional claim by Galba's lawyer. If the local judge were sitting, a lot of time and wrangling might be saved.

Herminius listened politely to Severus' brief summary of the progress of the case, but just as politely declined to join him on the Tribunal. The position of the Urban Prefect of the Baiae court, said Herminius, was that Severus had no jurisdiction and until the Bureau of Judicial Affairs in Rome decided otherwise, no local judge would legitimize Severus' status by sitting with him. If Galba's lawyer made a jurisdictional argument, that was Severus' problem. But, Herminius said, he would send his own assessor to observe the proceedings from the audience, just in case anything useful to his own investigation of the Cyclops case might come out.

At precisely the time when the courthouse water clock signalled the third hour, Severus entered the courtroom and took his seat on the magistrate's curule chair, a low camp stool without arms or back. The chair was set on a low raised platform — the Tribunal — and was flanked by stools for his aides. Flaccus, the judge's legal assessor, was on Severus' right, while his court clerk Proculus was to Flaccus' right, ready to record the proceedings in Tironian Notes. Police aides Vulso and Straton sat to the left of the judge.

A statue of Jupiter Fidius — the god of Good Faith — whose presence was necessary for an official court, was set up on one side of the Tribunal, while a large water clock to measure the time allotted to lawyers' speeches was on the other. Judicial lictors stood at attention, each holding the *fasces*, a bundle of rods enclosing an axe as a symbol of judicial authority and magisterial power.

In front and below the Tribunal were benches for the parties, witnesses and lawyers, and behind them was the *corona*, the semi-circular area for spectators.

The judge surveyed the courtroom in front of him and didn't like what he saw. The front benches were packed with rich-looking Romans wearing togas and displaying the broad or narrow reddish-purple stripe, symbols of the Senatorial and Equestrian Classes. They ostentatiously flashed jeweled fingers at the judge and broad smiles in the direction of Galba, who was seated among them draped in a black toga, traditionally worn by defending litigants to show tragedy and evoke sympathy. The *corona* was filled to capacity with a motley crowd of freedmen and slaves dressed in tunics. Severus knew immediately that they were the hired claque of Galba's lawyer, paid to cheer him on by vocally showing support for his client and displeasure at anything adverse to his interests.

Galba's lawyer was fat, sweaty and agitated, just like his client. He made a great show of poring through a sheaf of documents and then grandly signalled a young assistant to take away the papers.

Severus opened the session by noting for the record that the hearing was to take evidence in the investigation of the murder of General Cyclops and then asked the lawyer if he wished to make a statement.

Galba's lawyer introduced himself as Decimus Ambibulus, advocate for the Procurator Titus Vibius Galba. He then straightened his toga, took an orator's stance and with a studied and dramatic sweep of an arm, began.

"In all serious cases, I am accustomed to being moved to greater anxiety by the beginning of my speech than seems to be warranted by my experience and years. And in this present case, because I am defending a procurator of Rome, I have so many reasons for anxiety because the enthusiasm I derive from my absolute confidence in his cause is counterbalanced by the nervousness I cannot help feeling..."

"*Merda!*— shit," said Severus to himself when he heard the opening. He turned to Flaccus and whispered. "This may take all day." Flaccus whispered back. "It probably will. The beginning sounds familiar too. I think he stole it straight from Cicero."

Ambibulus explained at some length that he was nervous because his orator's art might not be good enough to extol properly the high virtue of his client.

"Don't be nervous, Ambibulus." "No. Ambibulus, you can do it," called two members of his claque in encouragement.

Ambibulus took up the challenge. With an array of superlatives, he gave a speech comparing Galba to various heroes of Rome's past, emphasizing his client's respectability, his status, his honesty, his virtues and his job and salary. Each virtue was accompanied by applause from the claque and vigorous head nodding by the *honestiores* seated on the front benches. "That's telling him, Ambibulus," shouted one of the *humiliores* in the claque. "Galba is honest," shouted another. The loudest cheer greeted the lawyer's mention of the procurator's 100,000 sesterces salary. It drew a standing ovation.

Severus whispered to Flaccus. "No one can stop a Roman court crowd from commenting, but this is ridiculous."

Ambibulus then reached what he described as "the most important point at issue" — the judge's jurisdiction to hold the hearing. He pointed out in somber tones that jurisdiction was sacred to the law, almost of religious significance, and then dramatically pulled a scroll from his toga and unrolled a map of Italy to display that they were more than 100 miles from Rome.

"You have no jurisdiction," he concluded.

Then he put down the map, put his thumb and forefinger together in an oratoric gesture of refutation and said with vehemence, "You have no jurisdiction."

"You have no jurisdiction," echoed a legal scholar from the *corona*. "The sanctity of Roman law is disgraced," called another. "The gods are shamed," groaned another, hiding his eyes with his arm. Three members of the claque moaned in unison. The senators and equestrians glared hostilely at the judge. Galba grinned.

Severus had enough. He interrupted icily. "If, Ambibulus, you bothered to read the authorizing documents on file in this courthouse, you would know the basis of my jurisdiction. I will not listen to any more argument on the point. This is a murder investigation in which I expect cooperation, not obstruction. Your client has relevant information and I want to have it. I'm interested in evidence, not speeches."

"Did you hear that?" commented a member of the claque. "The judge chastised Ambibulus." "What kind of court is this?" shouted another holding his hands to his head. Grumbling filled the courtroom.

"And another thing," said Severus looking directly at the lawyer, his tone rising and becoming vicious, his voice echoing through the marbled courtroom, and his eyes glaring. "Your claque is out of control. This is a law court, not a cattle market. I'm declaring a one water-clock recess, a third of an hour, and when I get back I want the hearing to proceed in an orderly fashion. Pliny has said that the first duty of a magistrate is patience. But you have gone too far. Do you understand me, Ambibulus?"

Severus stood up and stalked from the courtroom, his aides stalking out after him. Ambibulus and the *honestiores* in the front rows gaped silently, but the claque retained the presence of mind to hoot.

"That lawyer shouldn't be allowed in a courtroom," said Proculus when they were all in the judge's chambers.

"The whole claque should be arrested under the *stellionatus* statute for 'acting like lizards'," said Flaccus.

"It's Galba's doing," commented Vulso. "You should use the 'smoke' the *curiosi* gave us about his background. That would wipe the grin off his face."

"I didn't intend to," replied Severus. "After all, it's not really relevant how his family made their money. On the other hand," smiled Severus, "he has tried to degrade the court by his tactics, so why shouldn't I degrade him in return and 'return like for like', as they say."

"Do it," counseled Straton. "Fling him on the rocks."

"We'll see what happens when we return," said Severus.

"You have one water-clock to finish your remarks, Ambibulus," said Severus when he resumed his place on the Tribunal. "Then I will call Galba as a witness. Proculus, start the water clock."

The claque murmured lowly, although they glared as hard as they could.

Ambibulus was also somewhat more subdued, but as he began to speak again — this time on the subject of the harassment of Galba and his daughter by a judge from another city — his rhetoric took over and he droned on and on. Severus cut him off in mid-sentence at the exact moment the water-clock emptied.

"Galba to the Tribunal," called the court clerk.

The procurator took his place before the judge, accompanied by a renewed burst of applause from the claque. Severus silenced them with an angry glare.

"Though this is only an investigative hearing, and not a trial," began the judge, "I expect my questions to be answered truthfully and fully. Now, state your name and status in society."

Galba answered. "I am Titus Vibius Galba of the Equestrian Order and I protest this hearing. You have no juri..."

Severus and Vulso exchanged looks. Vulso was amused; Severus was livid.

"Was your father born to the Equestrian Order?"

"No, but..."

"How did your family make the money to qualify you for the Equestrian Class?"

"In business. And I don't see..."

"What business?"

Galba took a handkerchief from his toga and began to mop his brow. "Buying and selling."

"Buying and selling what?"

Galba answered under his breath.

"Louder. The court clerk couldn't hear it."

"Slaves," said Galba, looking at the floor.

"Your family is engaged in the slave trade? Is that correct?"

"No...yes...some of them."

"What kind of slaves?" asked the judge maliciously.

Galba answered into the floor. No one heard him.

"What kind?" asked Severus, raising his voice.

"For the...for the arena."

All the *honestiores* in the front benches looked shocked. "I didn't know that," one of them said a little too loudly.

"Now," asked the judge, feeling Galba was properly humiliated without also bringing up the selling of female slaves to brothels, "I want to know when you first met General Cyclops, where it was, and under what circumstances. Then I want to know all the other times you met him."

The audience only murmured its displeasure.

"He had the villa next to mine in Baiae, but the first time I met him was in the army during the Jewish revolt in Hadrian's time."

Galba mopped his brow again. "I was the...He was falsely accused of desertion. I was the judge at the

court-martial. The evidence was overwhelming in his favor. That's all I remember."

"What do you mean, that's all you remember? I want
the facts of the case."

"I don't remember them," answered Galba. "There
must be a file someplace. It was almost 30 years ago. I
don't remember now."

"Are you telling me that you remember nothing else
about the case?" The tone of the judge's question was
filled with disbelief.

Galba reconsidered. "I remember it concerned a
temple. Pagan temples all over the country were being
sacked by rebels in those days. It was near the beginning
of the revolt. Cyclops was on patrol and was taken prisoner and escaped. I remember that. He was innocent of
desertion. He told the court-martial what happened. My
judicial assessor agreed he was innocent."

"What happened to the other members of Cyclops'
patrol?"

"They were killed by the rebels. We found their
bodies."

Severus looked at Vulso, who looked puzzled.

"What temple was it that was sacked?"

"I don't remember. Some Syrian cult or other —
Magna Mater, Atargatis — I don't know which one now.
They're all the same to me anyway."

"Who testified at the court-martial besides Cyclops?"

"How can I remember that now. All I know is that we
found the bodies of his patrol. His story was true."

"Who was the judicial assessor who agreed with you
about the verdict?"

"I don't know."

"You don't know? Didn't you choose someone you knew, a friend or colleague, to sit with you on the case? Who was it?"

"I don't remember. Everything was irregular in those days. I wasn't even with the legions. I was just a civil servant concerned with provincial taxes. That was my regular job. But they needed people to sit on court-martials. There were so many of them, the tribunes couldn't handle them all."

"That doesn't answer the question," said Severus sharply. "Didn't you select your own assessor? If you didn't, who did?"

"I don't know. I think he may have been assigned to me," replied Galba, mopping his brow. "I don't remember who he was."

Severus stared at him for a long moment.

"Who chose you to be the judge in Cyclops' case?" He asked the question with a sharp edge to his voice. The claque couldn't repress a collective groan on Galba's behalf. Someone invoked the gods. Severus ignored it, keeping his gaze fixed on Galba.

'I don't remember. I was chosen, that's all. Someone on the legion staff. Whoever makes those appointments. The tribune in charge of legionary legal affairs, I suppose."

"What was his name?"

"I don't remember now. It must be in the records somewhere."

"When was the next time you saw Cyclops after the conclusion of the trial?"

"Here, in Baiae. This summer. He had the villa next to mine, as I said."

"Didn't you recognize each other? Did you remind him of the trial?"

"No...I...We...I didn't recognize him. He didn't remember me. We didn't discuss it."

"You didn't recognize him?" asked Severus in disbelief. "How many one-eyed soldiers named Cyclops do you know?"

A few of the claque forgot themselves and laughed. Others remembered and moaned.

"No others. I didn't mean I didn't recognize him. I did recognize him. But I didn't remind him of the trial. I only spoke to him once or twice if we met on the road or at the beach. Only to say hello or talk about the weather."

"I understand your daughter saw a lot more of him than that. Did you tell her about the court-martial?"

The senators and equestrians in the front row were now concentrating their glances on the floor and walls. A few of the claque giggled. The lawyer Ambibulus turned around and glared at his employees.

"I didn't tell her. She does as she pleases anyway."

"Your daughter told me that you advised her to withhold information about Cyclops from Judge Herminius. Why did you do that?"

"I didn't think it was important. Maybe I made a mistake. She told you about it, so no harm was done."

Severus and Flaccus engaged in a whispered conversation.

"You say the evidence at the court-martial was overwhelming in Cyclops' favor, is that right? There was no doubt about it. He was not a deserter. He didn't rob the temple?"

"Yes. It was absolutely clear. We found the bodies of his patrol."

"Then who accused him of desertion and for what reason? Why was he brought to trial in the first place?"

Galba gasped out an answer.

"What did you say?" prodded the judge.

"I'm not sure," said Galba, a little louder. "Someone didn't like him. It was a malicious charge. Someone had a grudge against him. In fact I remember being told that after the trial the accuser was convicted of bringing false charges against a superior officer and punished. There was bad blood between them."

"What was his name?"

"I don't remember." Galba paused and mopped his brow. "But he got a nickname because of the feud with Cyclops."

"What was it?"

"Odysseus."

"Odysseus!" repeated Severus sharply. "Didn't your daughter tell you Cyclops had recently seen someone he called Odysseus at the Crater?"

"Yes."

"Why didn't you report this to Judge Herminius? You knew he was investigating the murder. Why didn't you report what you knew?"

Galba had no answer. He just looked at the floor. There was a long pause.

"What did this Odysseus look like? Describe him."

"I can't. I would if I could, but I don't remember now."

"Was he tall or short? What province was he from? What was his army rank? I want to know about him."

"I don't remember. I've told you all I know."

Severus glared angrily at the procurator.

"When was the last time you saw General Cyclops alive?"

"A few days before it happened. I saw him on the beach. That's all. I just said hello. He was on his way home from swimming and I had just arrived to go swimming."

"Now, Procurator," said Severus, "I want you to go home and think some more about your answers here today. I will tell you right now that I don't think you have been completely cooperative, for reasons best known to yourself. Meanwhile, a full transcript of this hearing will be prepared, word for word. When I send it to Rome, I'm sure the Prefect of the City will read it with interest and perhaps so will your superior, the Praepositus of the Bureau of the Treasury. They will judge the extent of your cooperation. I suggest it will be in your interest to amplify your answers before my report is sent to Rome."

With that, the judge rose and left the court. His entourage followed him out. There were no catcalls.

SCROLL IV

XI

A NIGHT ON A PLEASURE BOAT

It was a beautiful summer night, the sea was calm, the sky clear and bright with stars and the Milky Way sparkled across the heavens. Judge Severus, his wife and aides, reclined on couches at the stern of a pleasure boat gliding effortlessly on the bay. A small orchestra of flutes and lyres played for the entertainment of the party while slaves served food and wine. The boat was illumined by torches, lanterns and the light of a silver moon. Songs wafted over the water from other pleasure barges and sometimes laughter or giggles or joyful shrieks could be heard, while torchlight from other boats created spots with soft, peaceful glows on the water.

The barge party was intended to discuss the Cyclops case, but the talk first turned more naturally to contemplation of the heavens.

"It was on a night like this," said Severus, "when I was a boy that I first fell in love with the stars. So beautiful, so mysterious, so far away."

"They're fire," said Alexander, "or so Plato thought."

"Or divine intelligences," added Artemisia, "as others think."

"How far away are they?" asked Flaccus. "Does anyone know?"

"No." Severus answered. "Natural philosophers can use geometry and mathematics to reliably measure the circumference of the Earth and the distance to the Moon, maybe even to the Sun, but the planets and stars are just too far away. Still attempts have been made and recently Ptolemy of Alexandria thought up a new way. It's controversial but he arrived a figure of at least 80 million miles away for the sphere of the stars. However, Archimedes a few hundred years ago calculated the sphere of stars at about 400 million Earth radii – that works out to more than a trillion miles, that's a million times a million miles. So really no one knows."

"Either way, the figures are staggering," said Artemisia looking skyward. "Millions and millions of miles, it's much more awe inspiring than the myths."

"If the stars are so far away," said Flaccus, "then they must move incredibly fast to circle the Earth every day."

"*If* they circle the Earth," interjected Alexander.

"Yes, if," said Severus. "Seneca wrote in his *Natural Questions* 100 years ago that whether the Earth stands still and the heavens move or whether the heavens stand still and the Earth moves is the greatest unsolved problem in astronomy. It still is."

"But," commented Flaccus, "it look like the Sun goes around the Earth, doesn't it? Just look at the daytime sky. We can see that the Sun moving, rising in the east and setting in the west."

"Yes, it does look that way," agreed Severus. "But how would it look if it were the other way around. If the Earth turned on its axis and moved around the Sun while the Sun stood still, as the school of Aristarchus believes?"

There was a stymied silence. "How?" asked three people at once.

"The same," answered Severus. "Astronomers have realized that it would look the same either way! The same to a person standing on a rotating Earth that circles the Sun as to someone standing on an Earth that doesn't move at all. So the way it looks doesn't solve the problem of whether the Earth stands still or the heavens stand still."

"Of course, there are a number of other reasons to believe it's the Earth that stands still," argued Alexander. "For instance, why, if the Earth moves, doesn't it move out from underneath an arrow shot straight up into the air? That arrow should fall back behind the bowman who is standing on a moving Earth. But it doesn't, the arrow falls back in the same place. That implies the Earth doesn't move and Aristarchus is wrong."

Everyone shrugged.

"Is it true that the stars make music when they move?" asked Straton.

"Not just the stars," said Artemisia, "but all the heavenly bodies. When they move, the movement itself produces sound, and together they produce a universal harmony — the music of the spheres."

They all fell into silence and listened, but heard only the music from flutes and lyres on deck. They gazed at the heavens until Vulso brought them back to Earth.

"Galba is lying," he said bluntly. "Cyclops robbed that temple and his patrol helped him."

"How can you be so sure?" asked Straton.

"His sudden wealth. Shortly after the incident he became a member of the Equestrian Class and a tribune. He suddenly had the 400,000 sesterces to qualify as an Equestrian. And that's not all."

Vulso then described finding the duty rosters of the men in Cyclops' patrol. "Candidus worked in the army documents section, Herculanus in transport, and Gaianus in the mint. I don't think this is any coincidence. I think Cyclops deliberately chose the members of his patrol because of their expertise.

"Look at it this way. If Cyclops was going to rob that temple of all its gold and silver and bronze treasures, he would have to arrange to carry it away and then dispose of it.

"Herculanus, who was with the vehicles section of the legion, could have been a wagon driver who could easily procure and use a large army supply wagon without any questions being asked. Then Candidus was with the documents section. He could easily get or make travel passes for Herculanus' vehicle, authorizing him, for instance, to drive right out of the war zone — to Syria, maybe. The army documents would get him through road-blocks without being searched.

"And then there is Gaianus, who worked in the mint in Alexandria. He's a very interesting choice for a patrol. He would be familiar with the process of melting down metals and coining them. He might even have been able to steal actual coin dies or procure used and discarded dies. I'll wager," Vulso concluded with a flourish, "that they literally coined money with the treasures they stole from that temple!"

"It's an interesting theory," commented Alexander. "But Galba said the bodies of the patrol had been found. How could they be coining money in Syria when they were lying dead in Judaea."

"I don't believe they were killed. Or if they were Cyclops may have had other confederates. I can't answer your question, Alexander, but I can feel it in my bones. Cyclops robbed that temple."

"There's another puzzle about the court-martial," added Severus. "Why it occurred at all. If Cyclops' story was corroborated by the bodies of his patrol and if, as Galba said, Cyclops was completely innocent, why was he court-martialed in the first place?"

"Galba said that someone nicknamed Odysseus accused him out of malice," interjected Proculus.

Vulso sneered. "A soldier of the ranks accusing a centurion of desertion with no evidence? I can't believe that. What I can believe is that Galba is lying to us. Maybe he even killed Cyclops himself or maybe he's in league with this Odysseus."

"Galba is certainly a suspect," commented Judge Severus. "Everything he's done is suspicious. His evasiveness, his threats, those antics in court. I don't believe for one minute that he's forgotten the name of his assessor. And why didn't he report what he knew to Judge Herminius? And why did he keep his daughter from telling what she knew? No, Galba is lying. We'll have to break him."

"Too bad," said Vulso, "that he isn't a slave or that this isn't a treason case. Then we could have him tortured for evidence."

"He's a procurator of Rome and a member of the Equestrian Order," reminded Severus. "Torture is out of the question. We'll have to break him some other way." Severus started to get angry just thinking about Galba and their day in court. "He may think he's seen the last of me, but it's only the beginning."

Severus turned to his court clerk. "Proculus, did you bring a tablet and stylus with you?"

"I always have them with me, judge," he replied. He took out his tablet, called to a slave to set up an oil lamp next to him, and prepared to take dictation. The mild motion of the boat would hardly interfere.

"Marcus Flavius Severus says many a greeting to Quintus Junius Rusticus, Prefect of the City of Rome," began the judge. He stopped. "I think I'll send a copy of this letter to Galba. It will give him something to think about. And Proculus, on Galba's copy, make the salutation read, 'Marcus Severus to my dear Quintus.'"

The judge collected his thoughts and resumed dictating.

"In conducting the investigation into the murder of General Cyclops in accordance with your assignment, I have discovered that one T. Vibius Galba, a Procurator of the Third Rank in the Bureau of the Treasury has important information about the case. It is my opinion, however, that Galba has refused to disclose this information and refuses to cooperate fully with the investigation. A complete transcript of the court hearing will follow.

"I therefore request that you bring this matter to the attention of the Praepositus of the Bureau of the Treasury and, if you feel it advisable, to the Emperor himself.

"Since the Princeps of the *curiosi* has expressed an interest in this case, Galba's conduct should also be brought to his attention for whatever action he deems appropriate."

Vulso laughed. "The part about the *curiosi* will frighten him more than the mention of the emperor."

"Send the letter off tomorrow morning, Proculus, and have Galba's copy delivered personally to him by Imperial Post chariot."

The judge leaned back on his couch with a satisfied grin.

"I have another idea," said Vulso. "I suggest we hunt for someone else who remembers the court-martial. After all, Galba is probably not the only living person who knows the story. There must be others who attended the trial or heard it talked about in the barracks. I'll have to go back to Rome, though. I'll begin by asking veterans if they know anyone who once was with the Legion XXII Deiotariana. I'll find a few. Then I'll go from there. Maybe I can find out the real story, even learn the identity of Odysseus."

"That's an excellent idea, Vulso," said the judge. "Leave for Rome in the morning. Straton, you go with him. You can take my letter to the Urban Prefect with you."

"And what about Meherdates," asked Flaccus. "Isn't he suspicious and isn't it suspicious that he's connected with a priest of Mithra, a Persian cult? What's their role in this? Why, for instance, were Meherdates' jewels stored in the name of a Mithra priest, rather than his own?"

"We don't know yet. Probably the jewels were stored in the name of the Mithra priest because the jewels belonged to the Mithra cult, not to Meherdates. But they're working together for some purpose. We can have the *Vigiles* in Puteoli keep an eye on the Mithraeum, but we'll have to find Meherdates. So I've instructed the *Vigiles* in Baiae to canvass the villas to see if he tried to sell jewels to anyone else and to see if anyone else knows anything about him. And Vulso, since there seems to be a Persian element emerging in this case — Meherdates and now the Mithraeum, and since we're at war with Persia, I think you should also go back to *curiosi* headquarters and let them know about it."

He took a long drink of wine. "Other questions we have to solve are why Cyclops argued with Meherdates and threw him out of his house a few hours before he was killed? And why did he go to the beach at midnight with writing materials?"

Severus put his arm around Artemisia and they lay back on their couch, gazing at the Moon and the stars and feeling the easy motion of the pleasure boat. The soft music, the sea breeze and the lapping of the water against the boat was all that could be heard.

XII

A DAY AT THE BEACH

The next few days were spent waiting. A copy of Severus' letter to the Urban Prefect had been personally delivered into Galba's hands by the Imperial Post. Vulso and Straton had left for Rome to report the Persian connection to the *curiosi* and to search for veterans of the Legion XXII Deiotariana who might remember something about Cyclops' court-martial and his accuser 'Odysseus.' The *Vigiles* were watching the Mithraeum in Puteoli and canvassing Baiae in search of more information about Meherdates. Severus, Artemisia, Alexander, Flaccus and Proculus together with the children or in smaller groups went fishing, attended the theater in Neapolis, or just lolled on the beach, sunning themselves, talking, swimming, reading, sleeping and telling stories.

This morning it was the beach. Severus, Artemisia, Flaccus, and Alexander swam and basked in the sun. The children played on the beach with other children, mostly alternating skipping pebbles into the sea, building sandcastles, playing tag, and swimming, all accompanied by a lot of happy yelling and screaming, jumping up and down and splashing.

Aulus and Flavia held some sort of secretive conference together with some other 'chicks' and came running up to their father. "Tata, tata, can we go to Pompeii? Can we climb Mount Vesuvius?" They pointed across the bay.

Everyone automatically looked across the bay with dread. "No," replied Severus and Artemisia automatically and started to supply reasons and fears. Alexander and Flaccus joined in. "Pompeii and the whole area are buried." "There's nothing to see anymore." "It's too dangerous." "It's too unlucky." "It's filled with ghosts and spirits." "It's an evil place." "The mountain may explode." "No one goes there."

"But," said Severus to the children, "I'll tell a true story about what happened there. A story my grandfather Marcus told me because he was there in Pompeii on the day it was destroyed. The goddess Fortuna was with him on that day. He used to tell me about it when he was an old man and I was a child. No one who lived through it forgot it, or ever stopped talking about it."

"What happened?" asked Aulus wide-eyed.

"I'll tell you what he told me." Everyone turned attentively to hear the story. "It happened almost exactly 82 years ago, during the reign of Titus, in August, on the ninth day before the Kalends of September.

"Grandfather was a young man at the time, about 20-years-old and had come to Pompeii for vacation. It was such a beautiful city. He and a few friends had taken a villa in town. Grandfather said that for almost a week before the catastrophe there had been earth tremors, not only in Pompeii, but all along the coast, even here in Neapolis, eighteen miles away. But no one thought much about it. There had been earthquakes before, even a big one more than fifteen years earlier, when Nero was performing in Neapolis. The wells had also dried up in the days before the eruption, but people thought it was due to the hot weather. Besides, it was the week of the festival honoring the birthday of Augustus and people were crowding into the towns to enjoy the athletic games, gladiatorial shows and musical and theatrical performances. Everyone was in the mood for a good time and discounted the warnings.

"On the morning of the eruption, grandfather said, he felt an uneasy calm hanging over the city. He said he remembered the dogs being especially nervous and jumpy, barking and yelping. But as the Sun climbed in the sky and the streets filled with vacationers and local residents out for the festival, everything seemed normal again, and grandfather and one of his friends spent the late morning at the baths and then had a pleasant lunch at an outdoor cafe near the Forum.

"At one hour after noon, just as they were paying for their meal and deciding whether to go to the palestra and watch the Greek Games or to the theater for a mime performance, there was an incredibly loud crack, and the earth heaved and shook, and enormous roars, like the bellowing of giant bulls, seemed to come out of the ground. Grandfather said he ran to the first intersection and looked down the street toward Vesuvius. The whole top of the mountain appeared to have been blown off, and a gigantic cloud billowed straight up from the mountain, like an immense tree trunk, and then it spread lengthwise on top, like an umbrella pine tree or a mushroom, but alternately black and white and mottled. Then, he said, as he stood watching the awesome sight, the yellow sunlight turned brassy in color, acrid sulphuric fumes reached his nostrils, and a rain of burning hot pumice stone, ashes and cinders began showering down on the town.

"Grandfather said he then turned and ran away from the mountain. But he soon realized everyone was doing the same thing and the streets were becoming jammed with screaming, shouting people, panicking to get away, while the sky darkened and poured fire, the ground shook and buildings began to collapse. The street, he said, was littered with clothing, as men and women took off everything they had to prevent their garments from catching fire from the red-hot pumice stones. The rain of ash and cinder was so heavy that if you stopped running even for a few moments, you became covered from head to foot with them, and in danger of suffocating.

"He told me some of the horrible scenes he saw. As he passed by the temple of Isis, he saw a group of priests run out of the temple carrying sacks filled with temple treasures and holy objects. One large priest fell down, spilling gold plates and vessels. His companions stopped, picked up the scattered objects and set out again to cross the Triangular Forum. But then a row of columns from a portico crashed down on top of the group, killing several of them, while the gold plates scattered around. The remaining priests then ran into a house to take shelter, where, according to grandfather, they probably died from suffocation. Grandfather said that going indoors was the worst thing you could do, because poisonous fumes were everywhere and the ashes and cinders were building up to seal doors shut from the outside and smother those inside. The heat was also becoming unbearable.

"Grandfather, however, made it safely across the Forum, stopping only to pick up a pillow from an overturned litter. He put this on top of his head, in imitation of others doing the same with clothes or pieces of wood, to ward off the burning pumice stones, which never stopped pelting down. As he neared the city gate leading to the sea he had a stroke of luck. Passing a side street, he noticed an abandoned horse and wagon. The wagon was loaded with crates, but the driver was nowhere around and the horse was confused and darting first in one direction, then another. Grandfather managed to grab the reins and unhitch the horse from the cart. Then he rode the horse as fast as he could through the crowd and out the gate onto the road to the sea.

"Although he was one of the first to reach the sea, the scene there was also one of mass confusion. People were fighting each other to get into small boats, sometimes overturning the boats, while the sea itself tossed and swirled, sometimes running way up the beach and leaving sea creatures stranded when the water receded. There were also continuous earth tremors and cries of grief and pain everywhere. Many thought the world was coming to and end. Ash and cinders and burning pumice stone continued to shower the whole area, and though it was still only the middle of the day, it appeared to be the middle of the night. Grandfather remembered dismounting from the horse and staring up at Vesuvius. He saw broad sheets of fire and leaping flames blaze at several points, their bright glare emphasized by the darkness.

"A while later, the first of the warships from the Misenum naval base across the bay reached the stricken shore, and grandfather was among the first rescued. He said that later on, when the volcanic debris had built up along the shore, many of the rescue ships themselves couldn't get out to sea again. In fact, that's how Pliny the Elder died. He was Prefect of the Misenum Fleet at the time and led his ships personally in a rescue attempt. His galley was stranded overnight at Stabiae by the wild and dangerous sea and Pliny was overcome by fumes during the night.

"As for grandfather, he found two of the friends he had shared the villa with on the same ship that rescued him. But the friend who he had lunch with on that day, he never saw again."

Severus took a deep breath and let it out. His face was grim and he shook his head in sadness. After a few moments he recovered and got up from the sand, put on a small smile, extended a hand to his wife and playfully pulled her through the surf and into the water for a swim. Alexander turned over and began to read his book. The children ran back to play with their friends.

When Severus and Artemisia dashed out of the surf, back to their spot on the beach, Scorpus, their chief household slave, was waiting with a message tablet.

"It's from Judge Herminius in Baiae," said Scorpus. "The messenger who brought it said it was urgent and was to be brought to you immediately. He's waiting at the villa in case you want to send back a reply."

Severus finished toweling himself dry, took the tablet and untied the threads holding it closed. He opened it, read it and closed it slowly.

"It's Galba," he said to his wife and secretary. "He and two slaves went hunting yesterday and someone shot at them with arrows."

They looked at him expectantly.

"Galba took the first arrow through the neck. He died instantly. And one of the slaves was shot in the leg as well."

"How awful!" said Artemisia.

"Yes," said Severus with a bemused look. "It also reminds us of Odysseus, doesn't it? When he returned home to Ithaca he slew his wife's suitors with his mighty bow."

XIII

JUDGE SEVERUS INVESTIGATES A THIRD MURDER

Early the next morning, Judge Severus and his assessor Flaccus drove to Baiae to confer with Judge Herminius prior to examining the clearing in the woods where Galba and his slave had been shot.

Technically, Judge Herminius explained, the murder of Galba was purely a local matter and completely outside Judge Severus' jurisdiction, even as extended by "that document", as Herminius called it. But since Galba had recently appeared in court before Judge Severus and since there was some possibility that the murders of Galba, Cyclops and the *curiosi* agent Bassianus might be connected, "the courtesy of the Baiae court would be extended to aiding Judge Severus in any inquiry he might wish to make." To Severus that meant Herminius was looking for all the help he could get. The local judge confirmed it by trying to pick Severus' brain.

"When we first talked," began Judge Herminius, "we broached the possibility that there was a lunatic at large killing people in imitation of events in the Odyssey. Doesn't the shooting of Galba by an arrow add credibility to that theory?"

"There may be a lunatic at large, at least where Cyclops and Galba are concerned," replied Severus, "but most likely Bassianus was killed by General Cyclops."

"Why do you say that?"

"From what we learned at the Blue Oyster Inn about Cyclops' movements there that evening. He came in with a grim face, looking for someone. He went into the garden where Bassianus was later found murdered. He came out smiling, telling a bouncer that he had achieved success. I suggest that he came in looking for Bassianus, that he found him in the garden and killed him and then left. It fits together. But, truthfully, I can't be sure until I learn what the motive may have been."

"Then what about the man with the limp, the one you asked me and the Baiae *vigiles* to search for. Maybe he's the lunatic?"

"Maybe."

"And then what about this Odysseus mentioned at your hearing — the one Galba named as Cyclops' accuser; the one Cyclops told Galba's daughter he had recently seen at the Crater? Isn't it possible that he is our killer, perhaps systematically murdering anyone who had something to do with that court-martial?"

"Except for Bassianus, of course, since he had nothing to do with that trial. Otherwise that's also a possibility."

"And what about this Persian spy, Meherdates? Maybe it's him."

"Maybe."

"If you don't mind my saying so," commented Herminius. "I'm somewhat disappointed in your progress. You have a lot of theories, but no proof. You don't even have the man with the limp or Odysseus or Meherdates."

"You're quite right, Judge Herminius. Unfortunately, quite right."

Severus and Flaccus were provided with horses and escorted to the scene of Galba's murder by one of Herminius' staff, a local policeman named Eclectus.

"Galba was found here," said Eclectus, pointing to the foot of a large, shady pine tree near the edge of a clearing in the woods. "There was an arrow in his throat. He had two slaves with him, one in charge of the dogs and the other to carry the hunting equipment. Both ran, one into the clearing away from that grove of trees where the arrow came from, and the other towards it. The one running toward the grove was stopped by an arrow in the leg; the other slave was uninjured."

"Not exactly a hunting accident, was it?" said Severus.

"Not exactly."

Eclectus escorted Severus and Flaccus to the grove of trees the murderer had shot from. "It's a weird crime," said the officer. "No one gets shot with arrows. I don't know why not, but most murders are committed with knives or swords or strangling, something like that. Not with a bow and arrow."

They ambled from the clearing to the grove of trees where the arrows had come from. "How good an archer does someone have to be to do this?" asked Flaccus. "Shoot two people accurately and quickly."

"Pretty good," answered Eclectus. "But it's not such an unusual skill. A lot of people who live in the area or vacation here hunt bear, stags or rabbits. It's a local sport. Some like the javelin and some like the bow. Some like both. But a lot of people around here know how to use it. Galba himself probably could have done it. He was an ardent hunter. He particularly liked to shoot rabbits, I hear. I could do it, for instance," he added with a touch of pride. "With a quiver of arrows on my back, I can load and shoot fast and accurately. In the army, the archers take target practice at 500 feet. The distance here was barely 50 feet."

They browsed through the area for a few minutes, idly scanning the ground and the foliage. Then they returned to the clearing and mounted their horses.

"I want to talk to the surviving slaves," said Severus. "They're at Galba's villa, aren't they?"

Eclectus nodded and they urged their horses along the path back to Baiae.

When Severus, Flaccus and Eclectus arrived at Galba's villa, mourning ceremonies were already in progress. The place was filled with officials and acquaintances coming in and going out to pay their respects according to protocol. Litters, carriages and slaves were all over the front driveway depositing guests or waiting for them to come out. The judge and his assessor took their togas from the saddle bags and Eclectus helped them wrap on their garments for a formal entry. A slave led the horses away and the judge entered the villa under the branch of cypress which hung in the doorway to signify death within.

Galba lay in state in the atrium on a gilded couch. The embalmers had skillfully covered the arrow wound. Occasional outcries from the professional mourners rent the air, particularly when a new visitor arrived. Incense burned in large braziers near the body. The judge looked around, but didn't see Galba's daughter, Vibia. He did, however, notice the lawyer Ambibulus among the mourners. What was worse, Ambibulus noticed him, came over and gave the judge a sloppy greeting kiss. The lawyer had been eating garlic, Severus smelled as he tried unsuccessfully to shy away.

"It's terrible, judge. Simply terrible." Ambibulus ostentatiously quoted Homer. "'The fog of death descended on his eyes.' What do you think happened, judge? Judge Herminius interviewed me at my villa this morning but he doesn't seem to know anything."

Severus held up his hand. "I'll talk to you a little later, Ambibulus. I first want to see the surviving slaves. They're here, aren't they?"

"Yes. Septem and Octo. Octo is the wounded one. They're in a bedroom." Severus noted with distaste that Galba's slaves had numbers as their names. "I'll have you shown in." Ambibulus motioned to a slave who came running over. "Boy, show the judge to Octo's room. Is the doctor still with him?"

"The doctor left a while ago but the musicians are still in there playing." The slave turned to Judge Severus. "If you'll follow me, *eminentissime*."

Severus motioned to Eclectus to come with him and spoke to Ambibulus. "Don't leave until I speak with you. You might be able to help me." He introduced Ambibulus to Flaccus and left them together while he followed the slave.

Severus entered the sick room, a small bedroom without frescoes or wall hangings, painted blue halfway up the wall and pale yellow the rest of the way. Incense burning in a brazier in the corner filled the room with a sweet perfumed odor while a flutist and a citharist played softly. They were playing the harmony of the four tones, traditional healing music. The musicians halted when Severus entered, but a nod from the judge indicated that they should continue the musical medication.

The slave who showed Severus into the room softly told Septem and Octo that they had an official visitor. Septem stood by the bed where Octo was lying on his back, his left leg wrapped in bandages. He had difficulty breathing and was in obvious pain. But he spoke to the judge as best he could.

Septem anticipated the judge's questions. "I told Judge Herminius that I don't know who did it. All of a sudden, I heard a noise, like a horrible gulp, and I saw an arrow through the master's neck and blood spurting out all over from his mouth and nose. Octo and I stood up in amazement. We just stood there looking. Then Octo yelled 'run' and I ran away from the direction I thought the arrow came from. Octo ran toward it. I don't know what happened next. I'm just lucky to be alive. The gods were watching over me. Poor Octo."

"How did you happen to be in that clearing?" asked the judge softly. "Was it by chance?"

"No," spoke up Octo wincing in pain. "We went there to rest and have a snack. We always use that clearing when we hunt in that area."

"Who knew you used it?"

"I don't know. Everyone who hunts there uses it. We've hunted with large parties and everyone stops there."

"Did your master say anything about meeting someone that day? Perhaps in the clearing?"

"No. We weren't supposed to meet anyone. We just went there as usual to rest and have a snack."

"Who knew the procurator was going hunting yesterday?"

"Everyone in the house, of course, and probably the people at the banquet the night before. The master announced he wanted to go hunting just before we left for dinner."

"Where was this dinner?"

"At the house of Ambibulus. The lawyer."

"Who were the guests?"

"I don't know. I ate in the slave's quarters. The master and his daughter Vibia were in the *triclinium* dining room with the guests. We don't get the same food either. Ambibulus is like that. But I heard the master mention it when I was putting on his sandals. He said he had to leave because he was going hunting in the morning and wanted to get up early."

The judge thought for a moment. "How did your master seem yesterday. Was he perhaps wary or nervous?"

"No. Just the opposite. Since his appearance in court four days ago he had been restless and nervous all the time. He would yell at the slaves for anything that went wrong. But yesterday morning he was completely changed. He was even jovial, which is unusual for him."

"Do you know what caused such a change?"

"His walk on the beach," chimed in Septem.

"His what?"

"His walk on the beach. After Ambibulus' banquet. We took him home by litter and on the way he told the slaves to stop. He wanted to take a walk on the beach, he said. It was just down the road from here. And he went down to the beach and I suppose he walked alone for about half an hour. When he came back we could see right away that his mood had changed. He actually made a joke and laughed at it himself. And he was still all right yesterday morning, before it happened."

"Why was Galba killed?" asked Octo. "Why did he shoot me? We didn't do anything. I don't even know who did it."

"I don't know, Octo," said the Judge soothingly. "But I intend to find out for you. Get some rest now and you'll soon be better." Severus left the room, Septem trailing behind, while Octo went to sleep.

The judge rejoined Flaccus and Ambibulus in the atrium. "I'd like to speak to you, Ambibulus," said the judge, "but," he nodded toward the body of Galba lying on the couch,"I'm afraid his presence would..."

"I understand, judge," replied Ambibulus. "May I suggest my own modest villa. It's not far and I can arrange for litters with no trouble at all."

Severus nodded his agreement and Ambibulus went outside to instruct his slaves to make the arrangements.

"What did you and Ambibulus talk about?" the judge asked his assessor.

"I didn't talk about anything," replied Flaccus. "That windbag did all the talking. Or all the bragging, I should say. He told me how great he thinks he is, how much his clients love him, all the wonderful and expensive presents they give him over and above the 10,000 sesterces legal limit on a lawyer's fee. You know the type, judge."

"Galba dined with him the night before he was murdered. There was a banquet." Severus put his arm around Flaccus' shoulder and guided him into a corner. "There's something else I learned. After the banquet Galba went for a walk on the beach. Before he went he was nervous and jumpy, according to his slave, and had been that way since the court hearing. But after he returned from the walk he seemed normal again, even cheerful."

"I'll bet it was your letter to the Urban Prefect that kept him nervous and jumpy," said Flaccus. "But what changed?"

"A good guess is that he met someone on the beach. Cyclops met with someone late at night on the beach. I wonder if Galba also had a late night meeting with the same person."

"If you're thinking he met his murderer, just like Cyclops did, why didn't the murderer kill Galba there? If it's the same person who killed Cyclops, it would have been no trouble to repeat the performance. Galba is fatter than Cyclops."

"I don't know, Flaccus. It's just speculation that he met someone. He may only have thought things out and reached some decision."

Severus noticed Ambibulus signalling him from the doorway.

"Ambibulus is ready for us." They began to walk toward the door. "But if Galba reached a decision by

himself," mused Severus, "it's certainly a strange coincidence that he was murdered the next morning."

XIV

AMBIBULUS PROPOSES A DEAL

A mbibulus had organized an ostentatious procession to bring the judge to his villa. Twenty slaves, headed by a flute-player, marched in front of Ambibulus' eight-bearer litter, while two four-bearer litters, one containing the judge and the other his assessor, followed along. All the slaves who carried the litters were either Syrian or Cappadocians, Ambibulus told the judge, since "those people make the best litter-bearers by nature." Twenty more slaves brought up the rear.

Severus drew the curtain, settled into a prone position and let the rhythmic motion of the litter put him to sleep. He was awakened by the commotion of the arrival at the lawyer's villa. He rubbed his eyes, opened the curtains and was surrounded by numerous slaves who held the hem of his toga as he descended from the litter, stirred the air around him with peacock feather fans and show-ered him with compliments and deferences. The judge was called "*eminentissime*" at least twice by everyone

who came close to him. Ambibulus was the most atten-
tive of all.

"These statues," the lawyer said, pointing to the lawn
sculpture of gods and goddesses, "I had brought down
from my house in Rome for the vacation. I don't want to
be without my art works."

Severus could tell at a glance that they were matter-of-
fact Roman copies of matter-of-fact Greek originals.

"Of course," continued Ambibulus, "the insides are
drilled out to make them light enough for carrying from
the city to the country. Otherwise," he laughed, "half my
slaves would have hernias."

A slave threw rose petals in front of Severus' feet
as he approached the front door of the villa. Ambibulus
pointed out the box hedges in front shaped in the letter
"A". "For Ambibulus," he explained. Then he turned his
attention to the front doors of the house.

"30,000 sesterces. That's what I paid for these doors.
All of cedar wood. Naturally, I have even more expensive
citrus wood tables inside. You must see them, judge."

Ambibulus' wife came to the entrance to greet the
judge. She had advance warning of the judge's visit and
was freshly, rapidly and overly made up. She had thick
strokes of black eye shadow on her eyelids, cinnamon
red rouge on her cheeks and lips, and a glaze of white
lead on her arms and face. She looked like one of those
women about whom it was commonly said that "she
didn't sleep with her face, but stored it in 100 jars." She
also wore an enormous quantity of rings, necklaces and
bracelets and a large, expensive pearl in her ear. The excessive cosmetics and the adornments served only to enhance her ordinary looks.

Severus and Flaccus were given a tour of the ornaments of the house. They were shown mediocre wall murals which Ambibulus passed off as the works of great artists commissioned personally by him at enormous expense; two full size statues of Ambibulus and his wife which, Severus noticed on close inspection, were not the specially commissioned creations Ambibulus claimed them to be. Rather the lawyer had used the old trick of buying two cheap statues, having the heads knocked off, and then replacing them with the heads of himself and his wife. At least, thought Severus, the original bodies were an improvement on the figures of Ambibulus and his wife.

Ambibulus next showed them his bedroom where the bed was covered with gilding, the coverlets were of the finest Chinese silk and the mattress had been treated with expensive perfumes. It was indiscrete, said the lawyer, to show his wife's bedroom, but he assured them that it was even more magnificent than his. Next Ambibulus brought out a large gold box which contained his first beard. Then he had the slaves bring out the silver plate. Ambibulus claimed it was the work of Polycleitus himself, made in Athens more than 600 years ago, and it had cost him 500,000 sesterces. Severus suspected the copies had been made within the past few years in workshops in the Saepta Julia marketplace in Rome. But the copies were not bad and probably had been expensive, though nothing like the enormous price Ambibulus had claimed for them unless, of course, the lawyer had been totally fleeced.

The parade of furniture, candelabra, chests, vases, glasses and statuettes passed in a blurred view before the judge and his assessor, with both Severus and Flaccus being reduced to weak smiles and nodding in response to the assault of objects, prices and phony claims. One vase made of deep green fluorspar, however, seemed genuine and must have been hugely expensive. At some point, wine and a plate of honey cakes were brought out and Ambibulus and his wife, their hands clasped together, stopped praising themselves and their household and just stared at their guests, waiting for them to shower compliments over their heads. Instead Severus asked a question.

"I heard that the night before poor Galba met his fate he dined here."

Ambibulus took it for an interest in the cuisine of the house — a subject he had neglected to mention — and commanded a slave to fetch the cook.

"He's a famous Greek chef," confided Ambibulus' wife, "and you know how expensive a good Greek cook is these days. But we bought him at a bargain price from one of my husband's grateful clients. How much did we pay for Palamedes, was it 30,000 sesterces?"

"No," answered Ambibulus. "Don't you remember. The doors and my valet were each 30,000. Palamedes cost 50,000."

Palamedes, a wan-looking old man, was brought into the atrium and shoved forward to stand before the judge. "Boy, tell Judge Severus what you cooked the night of the banquet."

"It was a banquet for nine," said Palamedes. "My master and mistress and seven guests."

Ambibulus interrupted. "I wanted to make it for twice as many, but my wife convinced me that the traditional number of nine would be more cultured."

She confirmed it with a platitude. "The number of guests should not be less than the number of Graces, nor more than the number of Muses."

Severus smiled at her. She smiled back.

Ambibulus gave Palamedes a sharp poke in the back. The cook promptly spoke up.

"We had rissole of rabbit, stuffed sow womb, roast lobster with pepper sauce, peacock with turnips and a whole grilled fish in Alexandrian sauce."

"What a meal," said Ambibulus. "Next time we have a banquet like that, judge, you and your wife are invited." He told Palamedes to go back to the kitchen and wrap some left-overs from last night's meal for the judge and his assessor to take home.

"Don't protest, judge," he said. "We had meat slices in white sauce last night."

"You can have it warmed up when you get home," added the lawyer's wife, "but it's good cold too."

"I'm sure," said Severus, turning the subject to what he was interested in, "the company must have been as delightful."

"Most congenial," replied Ambibulus. "Galba was there and his daughter Vibia. You've met her, I know. She's a beautiful girl, but wild.

"Then there was Gallicanus and his wife," he continued. "You may remember him from our little hearing the other day. He was seated in the front row. A small man with a surly face, but very congenial. He's a local decurion — a town councillor."

Ambibulus' wife chimed in. "You forgot Cocceius."

"Yes," said Ambibulus. "My young law assistant Cocceius. You may remember him from the court too. He sat next to me."

Severus mentally counted five of the seven guests. "There were two others, weren't there?"

"Oh yes. The other two were Milo and his wife. He's a local building contractor. Low origins but very rich. He makes a fortune putting up villas in the area. He built Galba's. And this one. Charged me a fortune too. I won't even tell you how much." Ambibulus lowered his voice to a confidential tone. "I only invited him because Gallicanus asked me to. Gallicanus is thinking of building himself a larger villa and wanted to get to know Milo socially. If you ask me," he lowered his voice even more, "Gallicanus will get a new villa at very little cost and Milo will get a few contracts to build for the town." Ambibulus smiled broadly. "And I'll have done them both a favor, if you know what I mean."

Severus knew exactly what he meant.

"Perhaps," replied Severus carefully, "you can do me a favor too."

Ambibulus raised his eyebrows and smiled. "I would be most happy to oblige you, *eminentissime*, though, if it's about poor Galba, 'nothing bad about the dead' as they say." Ambibulus paused. "At least not until after the funeral."

"And then?"

"Then," said Ambibulus with a deep sigh, "the gods will be appeased and life will go on. Naturally," he added carefully, "you understand, judge, that the confidence Galba had in me is still of concern to his immortal shade, and with the laws of compensation in nature being what they are...," he let the sentence remain unfinished.

Severus stood up and tried to control his anger. Ambibulus wanted a favor in return, and no doubt the more corrupt the favor the more information the lawyer would tell.

"I certainly don't want to violate the laws of nature," snapped the judge. "On that you can be assured. When is the funeral?"

"Tomorrow night. He's to be cremated."

They walked toward the door. Severus suppressed his emotions and decided to give Ambibulus the impression that was willing to play along. Once outside, the judge guided the lawyer toward a lawn statue and away from Flaccus and Ambibulus' wife.

"What's your price?" asked the judge in a casual voice, "for everything you know about Galba, everything he told you in confidence."

Ambibulus raised his eyebrows and a toothy smile crossed his fat face.

"I'll think of something," he replied. "I'll come to your villa the morning after the funeral and we'll discuss it." He gave the judge a knowing look. "It'll be worth it. Galba and I were very close."

They walked to where the litters were waiting. "By the way," said Severus, "I meant to ask you whether Galba mentioned at your banquet that he was going hunting the next day?"

"He more than mentioned it. It was practically the only thing he talked about all evening."

"How did he seem that night? Was he in a good mood?" Severus was curious to hear how Ambibulus would answer it. Galba's slave had remarked on the procurator's bad mood.

"Galba had been, shall we say, a little on edge these past few days, *eminentissime*. Your questioning him in open court, what came out about his father's occupation, the fact that you didn't believe him, and then that letter you sent to the Urban Prefect in Rome. That was quite a shock for him. He was a nervous wreck."

Severus and Flaccus climbed into the litters and Ambibulus' slaves hoisted them to their shoulders.

"Do you know the Blue Oyster Inn?" called Severus to the bearers.

"We know it," called back one of the slaves.

"We're spending the night there," called back the judge. He motioned to the slaves to bring Flaccus' litter alongside so they could chat on the way to the inn.

"*Vale* — farewell," called Ambibulus.

The procession moved off at a fast pace. "How much money do you have with you, Flaccus?" asked the judge from his litter.

"Not much," replied Flaccus from his.

"Good. I don't have too much either. So we can't lose much at the gambling tables tonight."

"And what about tomorrow? Are we going back to Neapolis?"

"No. Tomorrow we're going to visit that building contractor Ambibulus mentioned. Milo."

"Why Milo?"

"There's something that's been bothering me for a while now," answered the judge. "I've always been troubled by the 'coincidence' of Galba and Cyclops having adjoining villas. Milo built Galba's villa. He might know something about those houses. And about Cyclops and Galba while they were in Baiae. It's worth a try. And the day after, when Galba's shade is safely in the underworld, Ambibulus will tell me everything he knows."

"What will you give him in return. He said he expected 'compensation'."

"As they say," answered Severus, "from whatever direction the wind is, the sail is turned accordingly. I'll just see what the weather is like."

"In that case, you may find him to be only a bag of wind."

"I find him to be that already."

XV

MILO THE CONTRACTOR

It was a beautiful, sunny morning when Severus and Flaccus left the Blue Oyster Inn. They directed their Imperial Post driver to take them to the contractor Milo, whose factory was just north of Baiae. Maybe Milo could provide information about the two adjoining villas occupied by Cyclops and Galba.

The salt spray blew in the air and the smell of the sea filled their nostrils, as the coach headed north along the shore road. It was a pleasant ride and the judge and his assessor spent it discussing last night's gambling at the inn. Flaccus was depressed by how much he had lost.

"According to Seneca," consoled the judge, "wealth is really poverty adjusted to the laws of nature."

"I would prefer," replied Flaccus, "that the laws of nature adjust themselves in some other direction when I'm at the dice table."

"It's only money you lost," said the judge. "Epicurus, the teacher of pleasure, used to observe intervals in which he deliberately ate the meanest food and lived almost without money. He wanted to see whether he fell short of full and complete happiness and, if so, by what amount he fell short and whether this amount was worth purchasing at the price of great effort."

"What did he conclude?"

"Epicurus and Seneca agree. Scorn wealth. You may possess it, but you must be able to live happily without it as well as with it. Regard riches as always likely to elude you. Reduce your needs to an amount that no unfairness of fortune or roll of the dice can snatch away. There is also pleasure in a simplified life, without money. In short, Flaccus, forget about last night."

Flaccus smiled. "You know, judge, I don't believe Seneca."

"You don't?"

"No. Seneca said that when he came to Baiae he had to leave the next day because he was offended by the excessive luxury. That's what I don't believe. I think Seneca had to leave the next day because he lost all his money at the Blue Oyster."

Severus laughed.

Milo's workshop was in a large compound where the sounds of hammering and stone breaking were as constant as the sound of the sea just across the road. When Severus arrived, the contractor was fuming. Even in the presence of a Roman judge, he could hardly control himself. They had barely sat down on stools under an umbrella when Milo jumped up.

"Did you see the litter that just left?" he asked Severus. "Did you see that, that..." He was too livid to finish the sentence. Milo was a short, muscular, rugged-looking man, with callouses on his hands, whose color, as far as the judge could see, was red.

"That was the decurion, the town councillor, Gallicanus. I showed him plans for a new public bath the town is thinking of building. Good plans. Modeled after ones in Rome. Small, but elegant. He asked me how much it would cost. I gave him a very fair price. 300,000 sesterces. Maybe another 50,000 more or less, I told him. When he heard that he said, what do I mean, more or less. How much would it cost? I told him I didn't know exactly. 300,000 is an estimate. Sometimes there are costs that come up. A contractor can't be sure. Then do you know what he said. He said if I wasn't going to be specific, the town council would enact the public works law of Ephesus for this project."

"What's that?" asked Flaccus.

"You don't know about it? Well, you're not an architect or a contractor. It's a law invented by towns to use against contractors, that's what it is. It says a contractor has to furnish an official estimate on public works projects he does, and then he has to assign his personal property to a city magistrate until the work is finished. Imagine! The city owns the contractor's property while he's working for the city."

"What for?" asked Flaccus.

"What for?" Milo seemed to begin every answer with a question. "To collect. That's what for. The public works law of Ephesus says that if the final cost meets the original contract, the contractor gets a decree voted in his honor. But if it doesn't, if the cost override on the finished building is more than 25%, the government won't pay it. They pay if it's under 25%, but not if it's over. If it's over, then the overage amount has to be paid by the contractor. And it's taken out of the contractor's property which the magistrate already has. And he's threatening me with it."

"Too bad," interjected Severus. "Now calm down. You're talking to a judge of Rome, not to Gallicanus. And sit down."

Milo sat and changed to a healthy pink. Severus thought of telling Milo that the Ephesus public works law sounded too lenient, just to see if he turned white or green, but there were more important things on his mind.

"I want some information," began the judge, "about the villa owned by General Cyclops. Do you know the one? In the Nero Pond section of Baiae."

"I should know it. I built it. And Cyclops didn't own it. I built it for Mummius 10 years ago. Mummius owns that villa."

"Who's Mummius?"

"You don't know Mummius? Titus Mummius?" He asked it as if Severus were a complete ignoramus for not knowing. "Titus Mummius is Baiae's best procurer and brothel keeper. He provides high class *lupae* —'she-wolves' — for high class customers at the Crater. His best *lupanar* —'she-wolf den' — is behind the Forum in Baiae." He almost sneered at Severus. "All the best people know Mummius."

"How do you know Cyclops didn't buy it from Mummius?"

"You think Cyclops bought it from Mummius? Then you really don't know Mummius. He's put his money in real estate, so that when he gets out of the brothel business, maybe he can become respectable. No. Mummius owns a lot of villas around the Crater and rents them. Mummius never sells houses. Only she-wolves, and that rarely."

"I understand you also built the villa owned by the procurator Galba, next door to..."

"That's the only one Mummius ever sold. The one owned by the Galba family. But that's because," he lowered his voice in confidence, "it's all over town now, so I can tell you, *eminentissime*, it was because the father of Procurator Galba — the one that was killed the other day — his father was a slave dealer and sold his best looking women to Mummius for his brothels. So he and Mummius knew each other personally. That's why Mummius made an exception and sold a villa. That's my guess."

Milo paused to reflect. "It's funny you should ask about that villa because I was at a banquet with the procurator the night before he was killed."

"You were?" said Severus, feigning surprise. "Tell me about it."

"That two-faced town councillor Gallicanus was there too. All these local officials are like that. Two-faced. But I suppose all officials are like that. Except, of course," he hastened to add, "the imperial family and yourself, *eminentissime*." He gave the judge a weak smile.

"Just tell me about the banquet, Milo."

"There's not much to tell, actually. It was at Ambibulus the lawyer's. There's another two-face. That Ambibulus. Anyway, the food was good, although the portions could have been larger, and there were dancing girls and music and wine and the usual after-dinner drinking, conversation and entertainment. The only thing I remember about Galba was that he talked a lot about killing rabbits. Hunting them down and shooting them. And his daughter. She managed to switch to a couch with Ambibulus' young law assistant. I forget his name. But when the dancing was going on, she and he were really going at it. I thought he was going to 'poke' her right then and there. They left early, before the banquet was over. Galba really gave her a dirty look too. I remember that."

"Anything else? How did Ambibulus and Galba seem together? Did you notice?"

"I didn't notice anything," replied Milo. "But my wife did. She always notices things like that and she can't stop talking about it. All the way home, that's all she talked about."

"What did she notice?"

"That Galba hated Ambibulus. She said that she didn't know what Ambibulus thought, but that Galba just hated being at that banquet and hated his lawyer. She said she didn't know why a man like the procurator let himself in for it."

"In for what? What made her say that?"

"The way Galba acted. Fidgeting all the time. Trying to avoid Ambibulus' questions. My wife always notices things like that at a party. You know, who really hates who. You could see it too. Galba kept making excuses to go. He was always asking what time it was, like he had a girl friend waiting for him. But Ambibulus didn't want him to leave and kept putting him off. My wife couldn't understand it. After all, Galba was a procurator and Ambibulus is a nobody. Sure, the procurator might go to the banquet as a gesture to his lawyer, but to allow himself to be kept there when he was anxious to go? That's another thing. But then, my wife says, it must be because he has slave trader blood in his veins. Anyway, Galba finally just got up and left, saying he not only was tired and had to get up early in the morning to go hunting but that he also had a splitting headache. My wife thought it would take a case of leprosy before Ambibulus would stop fawning over him."

Severus laughed. He had a taste of Ambibulus' fawning the day before. Then the judge got up to leave. "Thank you, Milo. You've been helpful. And also thank your wife. She's very observant."

Milo's eyes lit up and his face puffed and reddened with a mixture of pride and blushing. "I will *eminentissime*. I'll tell her everything we talked about. She'll tell all our friends."

Severus and Flaccus stopped for a leisurely lunch in an open air seaside restaurant. They stuffed themselves with oysters and were entertained by a family of street musicians who roamed the area playing for coins. There was a man who played the double flute, a woman playing a tambourine and singing and a young boy clashing small, palm-sized cymbals. They first played a popular song and then an old classical favorite. The woman's voice was quite good, the musical accompaniment in harmony.

"It looks like Galba left the banquet to meet someone on the beach," said Flaccus, "and that he was anxious not to miss the appointment."

"Exactly," said Severus. "Just like Cyclops also met someone – his killer — on the beach."

The street musicians began another song, to which the little boy danced in a circle around his parents.

"What's happening to the search for Meherdates?" asked Flaccus. "Have you heard from the *Vigiles*?"

"They made a round of various villas but found no one who was approached by him. Proculus sent a message this morning saying that he's spending today with Judge Herminius' court clerk. They're going to examine the private papers of Cyclops and Galba, or at least whatever was found in their villas after their deaths. He'll report tomorrow."

The judge and his assessor finished their lunch, gave a few sesterces to the musicians, and then left the restaurant in their waiting coach.

"I'm heading back to the Blue Oyster now. I want you to talk to Titus Mummius this afternoon about the villa he sold Galba. He should be at his brothel behind the Baiae forum. Find out about the villa and anything else he knows about Galba and Cyclops."

XVI

MUMMIUS THE PROCURER

Roman brothels and prostitutes had to be registered with the City Aedile. It was not that the government cared about prostitution from a moral point of view. It was all economic. Brothels and prostitutes had been taxed since the time of the Emperor Caligula, 125 years before and the proceeds always provided a tidy income for the government. For a prostitute, the tax was the equivalent of one 'trick', not a very burdensome amount, but there were a lot of 'she-wolves', not just in brothels, but on the streets, in the taverns, in the inns, under the arches of the stadiums and arenas. For Roman men it was not disgraceful or even looked down upon to go to a prostitute; it was not even considered adultery under the law. This was to encourage men to enjoy prostitutes rather than the wives of their acquaintances.

Brothels came in all varieties, from cheap to expensive, as well as those in-between. In the cheap ones, the customers came out smelling of oil lamp soot. In the expensive ones, they smelled of perfume. In the cheap ones, the girls took care of themselves, in the expensive ones, there were hair-dressers and water boys on the premises to take care of them. In the cheap ones, the beds were concrete slabs jutting from the walls and covered with thin mattresses. In the expensive ones, there were real beds. In both though, the rooms of the 'she-wolves' were entered through a door with a reversible placard that gave the name of the girl and her price on one side, and the word *occupata* on the other.

Flaccus was shown to Mummius' private office in the back of the brothel. Mummius received the assessor at the entrance to his office, but didn't dare attempt a greeting kiss. His status and profession were too low for a Roman Equestrian to tolerate it. To Flaccus, though, Mummius looked like a fleshy, flabby, puffy, used up thing. The word 'degenerate' came to Flaccus' mind.

"I'm investigating the deaths of General Cyclops and Procurator Galba," announced the assessor with a deliberate mixture of authority and disdain in his voice, "and I have information that you knew them both. In fact, that you owned the villa Cyclops rented and that you were a friend of Galba's father. Is this true?"

"Yes, *eminentissime*," acknowledged the procurer. "I handled the rental transaction myself. General Cyclops had a letter of introduction from Procurator Galba, as a matter of fact, and I let him have a good villa at a reasonable price. I have the letter in my files."

"Get it," ordered Flaccus.

Mummius ran to the door and shouted an order. The sound of someone having a crashing orgasm penetrated through the open door. Mummius returned to Flaccus smiling, clearly relieved that the law was interested in Cyclops and Galba and not himself.

"So you knew the procurator quite well?" asked the Flaccus, prodding for more information, though his mind was now distracted by the nearby orgasm.

"His father was in the same business I am. I'm a friend of the family. That is, I was a friend of the family until the procurator's father died. Then I was a friend when the procurator needed something like a villa for himself or his friends."

"I see," said Flaccus, picking up on the implication. "The procurator took advantage of you."

"That's right. He was always a spoiled child. His father loaded him with money, got him into the Equestrian Order. It must have cost plenty, with a slave trader for a father. But Galba ended up as a procurator at 100,000 sesterces a year. I wish my sons were so successful."

"Galba may have been financially more success-ful than your sons, but I trust none of them has been murdered."

"I suppose you're right, *eminentissime*. And also," he paused to lend effect to what he said next, "I've never had to spend half my fortune to get them out of trouble."

"What kind of trouble?" asked Flaccus with interest.

Mummius cackled. He was enjoying the interview now.

"I know a few family secrets. Old Vibius — that's Galba's father — often came to me for advice and help. It was years ago. His son was some kind of tax official at the time, first in Judaea at the time of the revolt and then in Antioch. It was in Antioch that he got into serious trouble."

"Did it concern bribery?"

"Bribery? No. I said it was serious." He lowered his voice. "It involved a capital crime, *eminentissime*."

"Murder?"

"No. Counterfeiting."

"Counterfeiting! exclaimed Flaccus. "What did he do?"

"I don't know exactly. All I know is that young Galba was accused of an involvement with a counterfeiting ring. His father hired a team of high-priced lawyers and sent them to Antioch. Old Vibius spread his money and threats around Rome too. He knew the background and a lot of 'smoke' about a lot of so-called *honestiores* who didn't want that sort of stuff known.

"Anyway, *eminentissime,* you know how it works. The lawyers made up stories, witnesses became uncertain, officials lost interest, old Vibius got the whole thing quashed. That much I do know, because he crowed about to me."

"Did he mention any details? Think carefully. It may be important."

Mummius took a few minutes.

"He said a counterfeiting factory had been raided in Antioch and that one of the workmen arrested said Galba ran the operation. That's about it. But it was strange that Vibius never said his son was innocent. He just complained that Galba was weak, misguided and easily influenced and that he had fallen in with someone venal."

"An army officer?" suggested Flaccus.

Mummius searched his memory. "I don't know. But I got the impression it was someone who worked with Galba in Antioch. A government aide, I think, though it could have been someone in the army. Vibius told me his son made him get the other person off the hook too."

"Did he ever mention this other person's name?"

"No. I never asked and he never told me."

The assessor stood up to go. A stunning, barely clad young woman came in and handed Mummius a papyrus. She smiled warmly at Flaccus. Mummius bowed deferentially and handed the document to the assessor. "Galba's letter of introduction to me concerning General Cyclops, *eminentissime*."

"Thank you."

"And now, perhaps, you will allow Ariadne here to give you a personal tour?"

"Of course."

Ariadne boldly walked up to Flaccus, kissed him passionately and led him by the hand to her room. She made sure to turn the outside placard to *occupata*.

Flaccus eventually left the brothel, drained but very happy. He reported to Severus at the Blue Oyster and gave him Galba's letter of introduction to Mummius on behalf of Cyclops and recounted the conversation with the brothel keeper.

"Counterfeiting!" said Flaccus, "Mummius said it was counterfeiting. So Vulso was right. And Galba was in on it all along. He and Cyclops were accomplices."

"But Cyclops was transferred out of the war zone after the court-martial acquittal, according to his dossier," replied Severus. "He may have started the counterfeiting with the fruits of the temple robbery, as Vulso surmised, but he couldn't have overseen it when he was chasing barbarians in Germania. Galba's accomplice may have been someone else. I wonder..."

The judge shook Galba's letter of introduction to Mummius on behalf of Cyclops. "Galba perjured himself in court too. He said he had no contact with Cyclops between the court-martial and his arrival in Baiae this summer. But this letter proves the opposite."

"Tonight is Galba's funeral," reminded Flaccus. "Perhaps we should watch him burn."

"It would be a pleasure. But Ambibulus is coming to the villa tomorrow morning to tell me what he knows and I want to hear Proculus' report on the private papers of Galba and Cyclops first. We should go back to Neapolis tonight. Galba will burn well enough without us."

SCROLL V

XVII

A MEETING AT *CURIOSI* HEADQUARTERS

Back in Rome, Vulso and Straton immediately reported to the *curiosi* about the Persian connection to the case. In addition to the information that one of the last people to see General Cyclops alive was the jewelry merchant Meherdates, whose name was Persian, now it was known that his jewels had been placed in a safe box repository by the Mithra priest Suren. Probably then the jewels were the property of the Persian temple of Mithra in Puteoli.

This added Persian connection threw the *curiosi* into a frenzy. There was a war going on with Persia after all, and the Persians, having made a surprise attack, were currently winning. Brennus, the agent with whom Vulso had previously met, immediately called a conference at *curiosi* headquarters.

The conference was chaired by Decius Licinius Valens, the Princeps of the *curiosi*. Also present were intelligence officers of the two Roman legions stationed on the Persian frontier – the XII Fulminata and the XV Apollonaris. They had been detached from their legions and assigned to *curiosi* headquarters in Rome. They were supposed to be knowledgeable about Persian affairs, just as other soldiers from other legions assigned to *curiosi* headquarters were knowledgeable on the areas their legions occupied.

Princeps Valens was new on the job, a political appointment with little experience in internal security and espionage and not sure of anything except his formal authority and who his superiors were – the Prefect of the Praetorian Guard and the two Emperors, Marcus Aurelius and Lucius Verus.

When Brennus had shown Vulso and Straton into the conference room, Valens had already thrown off his toga and wore a comfortable blue tunic with two red *clavi* and a red belt. The soldiers were dressed in their military uniforms, as were Vulso and Straton.

Brennus wore a plain gray tunic with a black belt. He was almost as tall, almost as trim, and almost as athletic as the princeps. But then Brennus was in his 50's and the princeps in his 30's. A career agent in the presence of a political appointment. The princeps had the authority, but Brennus directed policy. Although the princeps wasn't convinced of his own lack of genius and competence this early in his term, neither was he so stupid or arrogant as to forget himself. Brennus was confident of his talents, knowledge and experience. He was not intimidated by his superior, but he knew his status in society was not the equal of a princeps. This did not make him bitter or resentful — only cynical. The princeps opened the meeting by asking Vulso to address the group about

Meherdates, the Mithra priest and the Mithraeum. Then Brennus took over the meeting.

"We have to understand who we're up against. The Persian secret service is called the *spasaka* in Persian, the 'Eye' of the Great King who they call the Shah of Shahs. The *spasaka* is a much older organization and more experienced in spying and espionage than we are. They go back many hundreds of years; we are a recent creation, not even a hundred years old. We hear they brag among themselves that they were behind the assassinations of Philip of Macedon 500 years ago when he was about to attack Persia, and also of Julius Caesar, 200 years ago, when he also was about to attack Persia. We believe these boasts are false, just 'smoke' -- they didn't carry out the assassinations, after all — but perhaps they were contriving to bring about the same ends at those times by spreading around their immense amounts of gold. We don't really know; the Persians are extremely secretive. How secretive? We know that since the time of Augustus, with the end of the Republic and the establishment of the Empire, many things that happen are kept secret and confidential. People nowadays regularly distrust and are suspicious of all sayings and actions that are related to the policy of our rulers and their staffs so that there are many rumors about things that have never happened at all and many things that have certainly happened are quite unknown. If that is the situation in our Empire, imagine what it is with the secretive Persians.

"Since we are currently at war, Persian agents will be naturally trying to find out information about our war plans. Remember that even during the 2nd Punic war against Carthage, 350 years ago, Hannibal had a spy in the city of Rome who was reporting war plans to him. We caught him of course, but that spy did great damage. Do the Persians have spies in Rome right now? Very likely they do. And they also would have spies at the Crater because in the summer that's where many government officials are vacationing, where plans are being discussed, where there is a fertile field for espionage.

"So, to be safe, for security reasons, we will assume that this Meherdates and the Mithra priest Suren are Persian spies and Mithra temples are their lairs. Also since the jewels Meherdates was supposedly selling belonged to the Mithra priest, we can assume the jewels provided his cover story, enabling him to meet Romans with knowledge and find out what he could.

" We don't know where Meherdates is. We must try hard to find him. But we do know where the temples of Mithra are; not just in Puteoli, but in Rome as well."

"So what will we do?" asked the princeps tentatively.

With a smile and a tone of voice both knowing and malignant, Brennus replied, "We'll think of something."

XVIII

VULSO AND STRATON INVESTIGATE CYCLOPS' COURT MARTIAL

The day after the meeting with the *curiosi*, Vulso and Straton took up their search for a veteran of the disgraced and disbanded Legion XXII Deiotariana who might remember the court martial of General Cyclops. They began by asking older acquaintances in the Urban Cohort if they knew any former members of that legion. It was as good a place to start as any. Ex-legionaries, like Vulso himself, staffed a large part of the capital's police forces.

The first person Vulso spoke to, a senior centurion in the IIIrd Cohort told him that as a young man he had been with the XXIInd, but only when it was in Egypt. He had been transferred to the III Augusta in North Africa a few years before the revolt in Judaea. He didn't remember any one-eyed centurion named Cyclops, but he had heard of a one-eyed general named Cyclops who was recently murdered. He suggested that Vulso speak to a *librarius*, a clerk, in the record office of the Urban Cohort who, he recalled, was an older man who had originally come from Egypt. Since many of the men in the XXIInd had been recruited from around the legion's home base in Egypt, perhaps he would know someone.

When interviewed, the *librarius* said he had never served in the XXIInd, but he knew a fellow Egyptian from his home town, Tanis, who had been with the XXIInd in the Judaean War. He drove a fire engine for the 1st Cohort of the *Vigiles* in *Regio* VII, the Via Lata region of the City.

The next day Vulso and Straton found the fire engine driver at the 1st Cohort precinct. They talked to him amid a jumble of hoses, hand pumps, horses and bells. He said he had been with the XXIInd during the Jewish Revolt and when the legion was disgraced he had been transferred to the II Cyrenaica in the Arabian desert. He considered himself lucky. There had been many court-martials with the usual range of punishments — deprivation of pay and deprivation of campaign credit toward retirement, reduction in rank and Ignominious Discharge. There were also corporal punishments and, he said, even a few cases of the death penalty for deserters. Many men had been transferred to legions in distant parts of the Empire, like Britannia, far away from their homes and families. He didn't remember any one-eyed centurions, but a legion has over sixty centurions and he didn't know all of them. He did, however, know his own centurion, Ceionius, and he was now living in Rome in a slum tenement in the Subura.

"He was down on his luck," explained the fire engine driver, "so naturally he came to Rome. He's drunk and broke most of the time, but if you sober him up, he may be able to help you. I can tell you where he lives."

Vulso and Straton found Ceionius' apartment house. It was an old five-story tenement in a back alley in one of the worst sections of the Subura. Half the plaster and stucco facing was knocked off, exposing the brick construction underneath. The building looked like it was about to collapse, except that the mice were still there. City lore had it that when the mice left, collapse was imminent; if they were still there, the building was safe.

Dirt, grime and roaches dotted the walls and stairwell, and the heavy, humid summer heat seemed to bring to its fullest the odor of human feces awaiting collection in a vat under the stairs.

A slave-porter sitting on a stool in front of the building told Vulso and Straton that Ceionius had a one-room apartment on the top floor and that he was probably sleeping off yesterday's drunk.

It took some loud pounding to get Ceionius to open the door. But when he saw Vulso and Straton, both in full dress uniforms of the Urban Cohort, and when he saw the centurion's vinewood swagger stick in Vulso's hand and his centurion's helmet with the crest side to side rather than front to back, he instinctively braced himself up, and the pallor that lay over his face seemed to dissipate.

"Is this the residence of Centurion Ceionius?" asked Vulso in a respectful military tone.

Ceionius came to attention and gave the infantry salute — the side of the right hand to the forehead, palm flat and facing down, parallel to the ground. "Centurion," he nodded at Vulso. "*Tesserarius*," he nodded at Straton. "Come in. Come in."

The room was small and furnished only with a bed, a table, a few stools and a chest. Ceionius cleared the table, pulled the stools up to it and motioned his guests to sit.

"It's not often I get visitors," he said. "Not often any more."

Vulso put his swagger stick and helmet on the table. The table tilted, as if one leg were shorter than the other three.

"We've come on a very important mission," started Vulso, "and we think you might be able to help us."

"Nobody needs me for anything any more," said Ceionius. "I'll be glad to help if I can. It'll be like old times." A look of pleasure passed over his face.

"Centurion," said Vulso, "we're investigating a court-martial case that took place during the Judaean revolt. I understand you fought in that war."

"Now that was a war. Not just some patrol action against barbarians, but a full scale war. We taught those rebels a lesson, didn't we?"

"We certainly did."

"I don't know why they revolted," mused Ceionius. "They couldn't win. They fought well, but we have an army of twenty-eight legions, not to mention all the auxiliaries, and every man trained for years from morning to night. They had fanatics. I don't know why they revolted when they had to lose. They did pretty well though, I have to admit."

Straton interrupted with a kind smile. "Centurion, sir, we came to ask you about a particular court-martial. You may remember it because it concerned a fellow centurion. Perhaps you knew him. He had one-eye and..."

"Cyclops!" exclaimed Ceionius. "I knew it. I just knew it was about him that you came here." He slammed his fist on the table, tilting it. "I heard about it from the Daily Acts. Cyclops, that general that got himself murdered a few weeks ago. I said to myself, I'll bet ten gold aurei that it's the same Cyclops from the XXII Deiotariana. He became a general." A look passed over his face. "And me. I became a beggar. Do you know what I do now?" He asked rhetorically. "I walk the streets with a picture of a sinking ship painted on a broken piece of wood, as if I was a sailor who'd lost everything in a storm. And I beg for money. That's what's become of me. And that Cyclops became a general. There's no justice in the world, centurion, never has been."

"Are you saying that Cyclops didn't deserve to become a general?" asked Straton.

"Maybe he did," replied Ceionius. "Maybe generals should be like him. A thief and a murderer. Because that's what he was. Everyone knew it."

"What did he do?" asked Vulso softly.

"I don't know exactly," replied Ceionius. "But I remember the scandal." He paused to collect his thoughts. The sound of children playing in the street wafted through the open window.

"The legion — the XXIInd — was in trouble," he began. "Everything was going wrong. The rebels slipped poisoned wine into our mess hall and killed off almost a whole cohort. Other detachments were ambushed. We got the brunt of the fighting. We were in Egypt when the revolt broke out and were the first legion to be called

in to help the legion X Fretensis. They were the legion
stationed in Judaea but they couldn't contain the uprising
by themselves. In fact, they got booted out of Jerusalem
and had to retire to Caesarea on the coast to lick their
wounds. We were supposed to relieve them and put down
the rebellion. And we weren't ready for it. I'll admit it.
Too much easy living in Alexandria and no war experience. The same as that legion that just got massacred by
the Persians in Armenia.

"Also the Jews were fanatical fighters. They were led
by some religious fanatic claiming to be their Messiah.
Bar Kochba — Son of the Star — he called himself. And
they were ready for us. Even before the revolt broke out,
they had already armed themselves by a trick. They had
armorers who were commissioned to make weapons and
armor for our troops, and these armorers deliberately
turned out equipment with slight imperfections, so that
when our ordnance section rejected them, the Jews kept
them for their own use against us.

"So we weren't ready and they were. They cut us
to pieces. We lost battles. Everything went wrong for
us. There was talk of punishment for the whole legion.
The craziest rumors were flying around, like the legion
would be decimated, they would pick one of every ten
men at random and execute him as a lesson."

"That hasn't happened for hundreds of years," said
Vulso.

"I know. But people believed it then. Maybe it was
only a threat to keep us in line. But it made things worse.
Soldiers got to looking out after themselves and forgot
about their duty. There were desertions, lots of them.

Military discipline broke down. I've never seen anything like it."

"And Cyclops?" reminded Vulso.

"I'm coming to him. It's one thing for an ordinary soldier, one of 'Marius' Mules', to do something wrong. But it's another for a centurion. We're the backbone of the legions."

Vulso nodded in agreement.

"Well, Cyclops was a centurion. And he and some of the men took advantage of the chaotic situation to commit a robbery. They robbed a temple. But then they made a mistake and got caught."

Vulso and Straton exchanged looks.

"He got caught!" Vulso repeated.

"That's right," replied Ceionius. "That was the scandal. The men who were in it with him never came back to the legion. But Cyclops did. He made up a story that they were captured by the rebels and only he escaped. To prove it, he took a patrol to recover the bodies of the men."

Ceionius paused. The sound of someone practicing the salpinx came through the window in trumpeting bursts.

"Well, the patrol found bodies all right. But they were only decapitated corpses in Roman uniforms. And then the leader of the patrol, he was a sharp fellow, he noticed that the uniforms didn't fit too well, and there were other things, I don't remember what, but it became clear that the bodies weren't Cyclops' patrol. So the patrol leader arrested Cyclops and had him court-martialed.

"They couldn't charge Cyclops with murder because they didn't know whose bodies they had: whether

Cyclops and his men had killed them or whether they had just dug up three dead men and decapitated them. So they charged him with desertion.

"Everyone knew what happened, though. That Cyclops and his men committed a robbery. His men deserted with their share of the loot and Cyclops returned with his and with a phony story to explain everything. And for a while he was probably wishing he had taken off with them."

Ceionius gave a cynical laugh. "But that was before he bribed the judge of his court-martial."

"How do you know that?"

"Everyone knew it. Cyclops made no secret about it. I remember hearing it around that Cyclops even bragged about it.

"Anyway, after that he was quickly transferred out of the legion. It was too embarrassing to have him around, I guess, or maybe he just bribed someone else to give him a new post."

Ceionius held his head in his hands. "And he ended up as a general. He used the money from the robbery to buy himself status and a career. But I did my duty and suffered the collective punishment dished out to the legion. I got an Ignominious Discharge. I lost everything. Rank, pay, retirement benefits, my chance for Roman citizenship. I put in 12 years. All wasted."

He was becoming maudlin. Vulso interjected with a question.

"Do you remember anything else about the trial. The name of the soldier who accused Cyclops, for instance. The one who found the uniforms didn't fit. Was he nicknamed 'Odysseus' by any chance?"

"That's right. How did you know?"

Vulso smiled. "Do you remember anything else about him? His real name, what he looked like, what happened to him after the court-martial?"

Ceionius leaned his elbows on the table, put his fingers to his head and thought.

"I remember that after Cyclops' acquittal, this 'Odysseus' was accused of pressing false charges and made to undergo a humiliating punishment. He had to stand barefoot in front of Cyclops' tent holding a clod of earth in his hand. After that there was bad blood between them. There were rumors that they were even making oaths to the gods against each other. That's why he got that nickname. Everyone began calling him Odysseus. It was natural. Cyclops and Odysseus. From the Greek stories.

"Then Cyclops had him beaten up."

Vulso arched his eyebrows.

"'Odysseus' was found near the beach in Caesarea, under an aqueduct, barely alive. He had been jumped by three men the night before. Everyone knew Cyclops was one of them because it was his last night in the camp. The next morning, before Odysseus was found, Cyclops had left for his new assignment in Europe. The last I heard of Odysseus, he was still in the military hospital in Caesarea. It was said he would never fully recover from the beating. They had broken both an arm and a leg and he had internal injuries too. His career in the army was ended. It was said he would never walk right again."

"Do you remember what he looked like or what his real name was?" asked Vulso softly.

Ceionius nodded his head away in a negative gesture. "No."

Vulso and Straton thanked him and got up to leave.

"You know," said Ceionius as he walked them to the door, "I may be a beggar and have no money, but I still have my self-respect. Every morning, when I get up, I say to myself the questions and answers that the tribunes and the troops exchange when a new day begins in the camp.

" 'Are you ready for war', I say to myself.

" 'We are ready.' I say back to myself.

"I repeat it all three times. Then I go out and beg."

Vulso slipped a gold aureus into his hand and left.

Outside Vulso and Straton remarked to each other simultaneously. "Odysseus is the man with the limp."

XIX

A FOURTH MURDER

At the same time Vulso and Straton boarded a boat in Ostia to return to the Crater, a knock on Judge Severus' bedroom door woke him in his villa outside Neapolis.

"What time is it?" said Artemisia sleepily. "Is Ambibulus here already?"

"No. He's due in a few hours. That was Proculus. I told him to wake me at the first hour. He and Judge Herminius' court clerk examined the private papers of both Cyclops and Galba yesterday. I want to hear if they found anything useful."

Artemisia turned back into a sleeping position. "Remember when you see Ambibulus, that when Odysseus' shipmates opened the bag of winds, it blew them off course."

"I'm hoping this bag of wind will lead us straight to port," replied Severus as he stepped into his slippers and pulled a tunic over his head. "If Ambibulus tells me what he intimates he knows, we may finish this case and have full time vacation."

Proculus, the judge's court clerk, was waiting for him in the library. He was seated on a stool with a pile of wooden tablets on his lap, the top one already open. Severus plopped onto a reading couch and lay down, leaning on his left elbow. One of the house slaves put a platter of white bread soaked with milk and honey on the table in front of the couch, along with a bowl of raisins, olives and cheese and a supply of napkins. The judge popped some olives into his mouth and nodded at Proculus to report.

"To sum it up succinctly," began the clerk, "Cyclops desperately needed money and it's my guess that he was getting it from Galba!"

Severus sat up with a look of interest. "How do you come to that conclusion?"

"From papers, correspondence and putting two and two together."

"Give me the details," said the judge, reclining again.

For the next half hour Proculus recounted facts and figures from the private papers of Cyclops and Galba, juggling the wooden tablets on his lap like a circus performer. He explained how the general's correspondence revealed letter after letter asking him to repay loans or debts and how other letters from friends constantly offered advice not to waste money on gambling and women. And there was a series of fruitless exchanges with the army in which Cyclops claimed he was retired and demanded his retirement bonus, the equivalent of more than ten years pay, while the army took the position that he was not retired, only inactive, and not entitled to the bonus. In addition, there was no evidence of any income.

"He may have had some money buried someplace," concluded Proculus, "but whether he did or not, he always needed more."

The clerk then turned to Galba, explaining that although most of the procurator's private papers were in Rome, his vacation villa did contain a personal account book which, as a financial official, Galba by habit kept up-to-date and presumably accurate. The account book, said Proculus, ran up to the day before he was murdered and everything in it seemed normal and explainable except for one item — a series of unexplained payments in the outgo column, once every week, for amounts ranging from 750 to 2,500 sesterces.

"The payments start," said Proculus, "the week after Galba arrived in Baiae for vacation and end," he pointed to the tablet to emphasize the point, "the day before the Kalends of August. Cyclops was killed on the Kalends."

"So you think that these weekly payments were made to General Cyclops."

"I do," replied the clerk with assurance.

"Interesting."

Just before the end of the sixth hour, midday, Artemisia returned from a morning of bird watching. She found the judge and Alexander playing *latrunculi* in the library. Severus was winning as usual, moving the black and white calculi with the sureness of an expert.

"This is the third game in a row I'm going to lose," protested Alexander. "I can never beat him at it. He's always thinking four or five moves ahead."

"I saw a hawk," said Artemisia. "And it was flying from my left to my right — a good omen. Or is flying from right to left the good omen. I never can remember which." She looked around the room. "Has Ambibulus gone already? What did he say?"

"He hasn't arrived yet," answered the judge.

"That's rude of him. It's also foolish, isn't it, for a lawyer to keep a judge waiting like this?"

Severus slammed a piece down on the board. "I had decided on cajolery. Now I may use threats."

"I resign," said Alexander as he saw his position had become hopeless.

Scorpus, the slave in charge of Severus' household, entered the library.

"*Domine*, there's a messenger here from Ambibulus."

"What's the message?" asked the judge. "He better have a good excuse."

"There's nothing written. He asks to see you."

"Show him in."

Scorpus left and returned, escorting a young slave boy.

"Where's your master," said the judge, with a tone of annoyance in his voice.

The boy looked at the floor. "I've been sent to tell you that he is dead, *eminentissime*."

"Dead!" exclaimed Severus. "What happened?"

"We found him this morning. The *Vigiles* are there now. He was strangled. In the garden behind his villa."

Severus was stunned.

"He was strangled with a silver wire," said the boy. "The *Vigiles* said it was a silver wire."

"Thank you," said the judge. "You may return home."

The slave boy left and Alexander quoted a line in Homeric Greek.

"I know," said Severus. "In the Odyssey the bag of winds was sealed with a 'shining silver wire' drawn tightly around its neck."

"And someone," mused Artemisia, "sealed this bag of wind in exactly the same way."

XX

A JUDICIAL CONFERENCE

Two days later, after an exchange of urgent messages, Judge Herminius and his staff arrived at Judge Severus' villa. It seemed like a gracious and conciliatory gesture for the Baiae magistrate to come to Neapolis for a conference, but to Severus it meant that Judge Herminius was desperate for help. As for Severus, he was depressed by the developments. Artemisia, with a combination of objectivity and irony, had pointed out to him that after he questioned Galba, Galba was murdered, and when he was to question Ambibulus, Ambibulus was murdered. "Who are you going to question next?" she asked wickedly. Severus got the point.

The participants in the conference sat on chairs arranged in a slightly oblong circle, with the two judges at either end. Judge Herminius was accompanied by his assessor, a young man about Flaccus' age named Marcellus, by the police officer Eclectus, who had accompanied Severus and Flaccus to the woods where Galba had been murdered, and by his court clerk, who Severus had seen only briefly on his first visit to Herminius' chambers in Baiae. Judge Severus was accompanied by his assessor Flaccus, his court clerk Proculus, who, like Herminius' clerk, was taking down notes of the conference on a wax tablet, and by Vulso and Straton who had returned from Rome the night before. Everyone was dressed in tunics, except for Judge Herminius who declined the invitation to remove his toga, keeping both his toga and dignity in place.

Judge Herminius opened the conference with a concession.

"I have discussed it with the prefect of my court and we have decided to withdraw our protest to the Bureau of Judicial Affairs regarding your jurisdiction. We welcome your help, Judge Severus."

Judge Severus nodded his head in polite acknowledgment.

"As a matter of fact," continued Herminius, "the Baiae Town Council had an emergency meeting yesterday — all 100 members — and unanimously passed a resolution calling for the immediate capture of the criminal. I have to give the Town Councillor Gallicanus a complete report on the case tomorrow. He was a personal friend of Galba and Ambibulus. I am, therefore, under some pressure."

Severus could see the worry in his colleague's face. Herminius turned to his assessor. "Marcellus. You tell them what's been going on." A look of displeasure passed across the judge's face when he thought about it.

"The significance of the silver wire has escaped no one's attention," began Marcellus. "Particularly after the Odysseus-like murder of General Cyclops and the bow and arrow murder of Procurator Galba last week. People also remember the death of Bassianus at the Blue Oyster and have made a connection. Some say the fact that he was bludgeoned with a rock refers to the Lastrygonians who hurled huge stones at Odysseus' ships, while others argue the fact that he was also drowned recalls Scylla and Charybdis, the rock and the whirlpool.

"The story of a maniac who thinks he's Odysseus is all over the Crater. I heard this morning that there's been a run on the bookstores for all available copies of Homer and a public reading of the Odyssey is to be given in the Baiae theater tomorrow."

"It sounds like the social event of the season," Severus couldn't help jibing.

"It may be to some," sniffed Judge Herminius, "but to others it's more serious. People are asking for protection. Everyone thinks they're next on the list. In Baiae alone, the number of women who think they're the nymph Calypso is simply staggering."

"What does he mean 'think'," whispered Vulso into Severus' ear.

Herminius became indignant. "I've even had two flagrantly effeminate youths come to my chambers asking for protection, claiming they're Scylla and Charybdis. A princess from Palmyra, who was on vacation from a diplomatic mission in Rome, packed up with her whole entourage because she got it into her head that she is the Princess Nausicaa in the Odyssey.

"People won't stand under cliffs for fear that the 'Lastrygonians' will hurl huge stones down on them. I have lotus eaters and hordes of suitors who claim they'll be next because they're chasing Odysseus' wife."

"Perhaps we should introduce the suitors to the nymphs," commented Severus.

Everyone laughed. Even Judge Herminius cracked a smile. "We've even had two false confessions," said Herminius.

"Yes?" said Severus, interested.

"Both were obtained under torture." Herminius turned to his police aide. "Eclectus. Tell them."

"The *Vigiles* think the murderer might be a maniac hiding in the hills who sneaks into the town to commit his crimes. We've therefore been scouring the surrounding countryside. Yesterday we called in help from the sailors at the Misenum Fleet Naval Base. Naturally in such a search we've rounded up a number of runaway slaves and criminals, mostly hiding in the hills. Those who are suspicious, we torture for information."

"Two of them confessed," interrupted Judge Herminius. "But they couldn't have done it. I questioned them myself."

"Why not?" asked Severus.

Eclectus answered. "They didn't know the right details. They were only confessing to stop the torture."

"What other lines of investigation are you following?" asked Severus hopefully.

"All theories are being examined," replied Herminius vaguely. "I am hampered by the lack of physical evidence. The murderer strikes swiftly and leaves no traces. Most likely all the murders were done by the same individual, though I have not closed my mind to other possibilities."

Herminius turned the question back on Judge Severus. "On that subject, Judge Severus, I wonder if I might ask what became of your search for the jewel merchant Meherdates, the one who had the argument with General Cyclops the afternoon before his murder."

"Certainly, Judge Herminius," responded Severus politely. "He has not been found. I did, however, trace him to a safe depository in the Tyrian trading concession in Puteoli. He was seen in the company of a priest of Mithra named Suren. The priest rented the safe deposit box, but Meherdates was with him."

"And what was in the box?" asked Herminius.

"I don't know," replied Severus.

"You don't know? Didn't you get a court order from a judge in Puteoli?"

"No," answered Severus. "It wasn't Meherdates' box and we have nothing against the priest."

Herminius thought a moment. "Perhaps I can stretch the law a little for you. After all, this is a multiple murder case."

He turned to his clerk. "Prepare a request to Judge Publius Manilius Carbo in Puteoli. He's a personal friend," explained Herminius to Severus. The judge resumed dictating. "Tell him I want a court order to open that box. Get the details from Judge Severus' clerk after the meeting. Tell Judge Carbo I want that box opened as soon as possible. Tell him it has to do with the 'Odysseus murders.'"

He turned back to face Severus. "Whatever is in the box will be in our hands in a few days, Judge Severus."

Severus made a gesture of thanks.

"And now, Judge Severus, said Herminius, "there is one other matter I'd like to discuss. At our last meeting, I presented the possibility that the Odysseus from the court-martial trial might be systematically trying to kill everyone connected with that trial."

Severus nodded. "It's certainly possible, although when you mentioned it I pointed out that Bassianus wouldn't fit in. Now I can add, where does Ambibulus fit in?"

Herminius had a ready answer. "Is it not possible that Ambibulus was Galba's assessor at the court-martial?" A flash of triumph showed on his face.

"No," answered Severus. "It's not possible."

"Why not?" asked Herminius, the look of triumph evaporating.

"Ambibulus wasn't the assessor at the court martial. I know because the thought also crossed my mind when I heard he was murdered. So I sent a message to Ambibulus' wife yesterday, asking if he had been in Judaea or Syria at the time of the Jewish war. She replied this morning that he has never been east of Italy in his life. He once had a legal job for the government in Gaul, but not in Judaea.

"Of course, it doesn't obviate the theory with respect to Cyclops and Galba. And that assessor, whoever he is, may be in real danger of being the next victim. But Ambibulus was killed for some other reason."

Herminius pondered the reply with a dour look. His assessor Marcellus took another tack.

"Isn't it possible that Odysseus and this jewelry salesman Meherdates is one and the same person? That Meherdates is Odysseus disguised?"

"No, it's not, because I now know who Odysseus is."

"Who is he?"

Severus then gave Herminius and Marcellus a brief summary of what Vulso and Straton learned in Rome, capsulizing their interview with the former centurion of the Legion XXII Deiotariana.

"I think you'll agree that the conclusion is inescapable. The 'Odysseus' who discovered Cyclops' crime and had him court martialed in Judaea, whose leg was then broken by Cyclops and his henchmen, is the same person as the man with the limp who exchanged stares of hatred with Cyclops at the Blue Oyster Inn in Baiae. The same person Cyclops told his girl friends, Galba's daughter Vibia and the Syrian dancers, who would try to kill him."

"Then what do we do next?" asked Herminius. "What do I tell the Town Council? They want results right now."

Severus shrugged his shoulders. "Tell them it's not a madman terrorizing the Crater in order to ruin the tourist season. The victims were chosen for specific motives, not at random."

"I will," said Herminius. "And I'll mention your name in my report. I'll give you credit. But they won't be patient."

Severus inclined his head in a polite gesture of thanks, though thinking to himself that Herminius was more inclined to offer him up to the Baiae Town Council to blame for failure rather than to credit for results.

"So this Odysseus has a very strong motive to exact revenge," commented Herminius. "He was the victim of a grave injustice. And it also doesn't reflect too highly on Galba," the local judge added wryly. "Bribery. I can hardly believe it."

"I also have information," added Judge Severus, "that Galba was at one time involved in a counterfeiting ring. He took over the ring started by Cyclops to launder the money from the temple robbery when Cyclops was transferred out of the war zone."

Herminius looked shocked. "Counterfeiting? The procurator? Where did you get such information?"

"From a friend of Galba's family," informed Severus, though omitting his source was Mummius the brothel owner. "The story is that Galba and an accomplice ran a counterfeiting operation in the East. They apparently turned the loot from Cyclops' temple robbery into coins. Galba's father paid huge bribes to cover up his son's involvement."

"I see," said Herminius with a frown. "More malicious gossip. My clerk even tells me that he and your clerk think General Cyclops was extorting money from the procurator. I don't believe that either."

Herminius stood up to go. His staff followed him. "And what's more," the local judge added with some asperity, "the Town Council won't believe it. I've got to have more than family enmities, vicious gossip or the wild imagination of court clerks to present to the Town Council."

Severus walked Herminius and his staff to their waiting carriage. The air was warm and smelled of summer.

"I'll let you know," said Herminius, "if anyone else confesses. Eclectus may be right after all. The killer may be hiding in the hills, even if he is this 'Odysseus' from the Roman army. But I'll instruct Eclectus to torture only those people with limps."

Severus stared after him. Was he being serious? Or sardonic?

XXI

A DISCOVERY IS MADE

Two days later Eclectus arrived at Judge Severus' villa in a swift government chariot. He carried a package with him. Scorpus, the slave in charge of Severus' household, escorted him through the villa and into the garden where the judge was lying on a couch, reading one of his vacation books, Lucian's *True History*. The judge was dressed in a light summer tunic, white with a red geometrical design on the hem and sleeves. A cool early morning breeze wafted through the trees and birds were chirping merrily as the sun warmed the air. Argos and Phaon were lying contentedly at the foot of the couch, each licking their paws. At the moment, the judge was on Venus, following the Sun people riding their giant winged ants to victory over the Moon people. What a relief from the case, thought Severus more than once. But when Scorpus and Eclectus interrupted the judge, it was back to reality.

"It's from the safe depository in Puteoli," said Eclectus as he handed the package to Severus. "Judge Carbo's court order. It feels like a box."

Severus thanked Eclectus and told Scorpus to call Artemisia and his aides into the garden. He then placed the package on a garden table. It was only a short wait until everyone was excitedly gathered around.

"What's in it?" said three people at once.

"I don't know," replied Eclectus. "Judge Carbo sent it to our chambers last night, but Judge Herminius felt that Judge Severus should open it, since it was your investigation that located it."

Severus nodded. "It feels like a box," said the judge. He then cut the string and began to pull off the cheap papyrus wrapping.

"It is a box," he said and pulled the papyrus off completely. There was no latch. The judge simply opened the lid and looked inside. He pulled out three leather pouches and a few rolled up sheafs of papyrus, motioned for someone to take away the box and placed the contents on the table instead. He then opened one of the pouches and turned it upside down.

"Jewels," exclaimed Flaccus.

"Are they real?" asked Vulso. "Who knows something about jewels?"

Artemisia picked up a few gems from the table. "They look real enough to me. Pearls and rubies mostly. A few other semi-precious stones. One's an amethyst. A few pieces of lapis lazuli. We should call in a jeweler for an expert appraisal."

"Arrange it Proculus," ordered the judge. His clerk made a note on his wax tablet.

Some of the household slaves had brought tables from the villa out into the garden. Severus opened a second pouch over a second table. Gold coins spilled out. A lot of them. He opened a third pouch over a third table. Another rush of coins, this time silver coins, covered the marble surface.

"Ah," said Flaccus, his eyes lighting up. "Money."

Vulso and Straton began to count and sort the coins on one table while Flaccus and Eclectus did the same on the other. Proculus stood by to record the results on his tablet. Severus gave a sheaf of papyrus to Artemisia while he began examining another.

"It's in Greek," she said while scanning the papyrus. "But it's hard to read the handwriting." She had switched to speaking Greek.

"This looks like some kind of business record," commented Severus, examining another sheaf of papyrus. "Memoranda of sale. It's hard to say. It appears to be in some sort of personal notes or shorthand or code."

"The same here," commented Artemisia. "I can make out a few place names, like Delphi, Corinth. Then there's a few letters. A theta. Maybe that's for Thebes. I can't tell. There's a lot of numbers too."

"We'll have to give them to Quintus to study," said the judge. Proculus looked over when he heard his name mentioned.

Severus noticed that Vulso was biting a coin. He had a quizzical look on his face. He bit another one and dropped them on the table a few times to hear the clink.

"What's the matter, Vulso?" asked the judge. "Did you find something?"

"Most of these coins look all right," answered the centurion. "Mostly Roman imperial coins. Gold aurei and silver denarii. There are also a few bronze local coins from cities in Greece and the East. One from Sicyon. Another from Tyre. Small stuff. But most of the coins are gold ones."

He extended his palm with three silver coins in them. "And then there are these."

Everyone had stopped what they were doing and looked at the coins in Vulso's hand.

"What's wrong with them?" asked Straton. "They look like ordinary provincial coinage. Greek silver-alloyed tetradrachmas."

"Look more closely," said Vulso. Straton did but without understanding what Vulso was getting at.

"It may be a coincidence," said the centurion, "but these coins — see, the reverse side shows the goddess of the Nile seated, holding a reed and a cornucopia — they're from Egypt — the Alexandria mint. And," continued Vulso turning the coins over, "the obverse has the head of Hadrian. They're from his reign. And they're dated," he pointed to part of the inscription, "to the year 15 of Hadrian's reign."

"That's about the beginning of the Jewish revolt," commented Alexander.

"It's the same year as Cyclops' court-martial," replied Vulso, accurately recalling the date on the document he had found in the archives.

"Are the coins counterfeit?" asked Severus.

"I can't tell for sure," said Vulso. "The metal seems good..." He left the sentence hanging. "We should send them up to the mint in Rome. They'll give us an expert opinion."

Severus turned to Proculus. "Do it immediately, Quintus."

Proculus called for a slave and told him to go quickly to the Imperial Post and bring back a special courier for a mission to the capital.

"Do you think these are some of the coins that Galba's ring minted?" asked Flaccus.

"I'll wager they are," replied Vulso.

"Then Meherdates must have gotten them either from Cyclops or Galba," suggested Flaccus suddenly.

"Let's not jump to conclusions," said Severus. "We don't know yet whether they're..."

"Here's something!" exclaimed Artemisia, still reading through the written material. "It may be very important."

Everyone turned to look at her.

"On the back of one of these papers there's a memo that looks like a booking on a ship. It says 'Triton.' Then 'Puteoli to Antioch' and then 'Kalends of September.'" She handed the page to Severus.

"The Kalends of September," said Proculus. "That's three days from now."

Everyone looked at each other. Grins broke out on their faces.

"One of them, Meherdates and Suren, or both are traveling from here to the East. To Antioch. To the war zone. And they have to be back here for the ship," said Vulso. "We've got them."

"Where shall we take them?" asked Straton. "At the ship?"

"I think at the safe-depository," suggested Severus. He pointed to the jewels and the money scattered over the tables. "They're not going to leave for Antioch without this."

XXII

MEHERDATES AND SUREN ARE CAPTURED

Judge Severus and his assessor Flaccus sat in the tavern across the street from the safe depository and forced down what seemed like their twentieth drink of the day. Flaccus rolled the three dice out of the cup and moved counters on a *tabula* board. He was about to win his second game of the day and pull even with the judge. The day before Severus had won all seven games of *latrunculi*. On this day Flaccus had insisted on switching to a game with dice. But he was still losing. Severus seemed to hit all his blots and when bearing off rolled too many triples.

"Maybe they'll never come," said Flaccus with a touch of resignation in his voice.

"They'll come," assured the judge. "Or at least one of them will. The jewels and money are here."

The same conversation, almost word for word, was being repeated inside the repository between Vulso and Eclectus, both police officers dressed in ordinary brown wool tunics like most of the employees or slaves of the establishment.

A team of police acting as idlers, pedestrians and shoppers covered the streets around the depository building.

The ship 'Triton' was in port, having arrived from Antioch two weeks before. It was a medium-sized merchant ship with room for about 200 passengers. It had unloaded its cargo of luxury goods, wine, oil, silverware, books, marble and other trade items and was taking on a varied cargo of manufactured goods for the return voyage, still scheduled to depart the next day — the Kalends of September. According to the ship's captain, only a report of rain squalls at sea or inefficiency by the port authority clerks could delay harbor clearance. Straton and a squad of *Vigiles* were posted on the dock and on the ship itself in case only Meherdates or Suren went to the repository while the other boarded the ship directly.

An hour after the *tabula* game ended, Severus and Flaccus were discussing the weather and talking about going swimming later. But then the subject turned to geography and then to history and then to literature. They were discussing philosophy when a police officer came to their table and whispered, "They're inside now, *eminentissime*. Both of them. We saw them go in."

Severus and Flaccus watched as the street was cordoned off and four uniformed *Vigiles* brandished swords and stationed themselves right outside the repository door.

Vulso and Eclectus also saw them coming in. Meherdates was recognizable by his oriental robe and square-cut Persian style beard; Suren by his priestly robes with the rank of 'Lion' symbols – a shovel, a thunderbolt, a laurel wreath and a *sistrum*. They both un-slung traveler's musette bags from their shoulders and put them on the floor. Petilius, the proprietor, had been instructed to act normally.

"May I help you," he said.

"My name is Suren," said the priest in eastern-ac-cented Greek. "I wish to claim my property from the repository." He presented the proprietor with a wooden token.

"I remember you," said Petilius, giving the prear-ranged signal. "Let me check the ledger."

He walked to a table and began turning pages of an open codex-style ledger. Eclectus sidled toward the door behind the men, while Vulso strode directly in front of them.

"Is your name Meherdates?" he asked directly in Greek.

Meherdates raised an eyebrow in a show of surprise. "It is."

Vulso nodded. Eclectus opened the door. The four uniformed officers entered with their swords drawn.

"You're both under arrest," said Vulso.

Meherdates and Suren saw the armed men. A look of confusion passed over their faces. The police started to search both of them for weapons.

"What's this all about?" said Meherdates.

"What did we do?" asked Suren.

Vulso looked straight into Meherdates' eyes. "You're going to a courthouse in the Forum where you will be questioned. If you want a technical charge, it's mur-der, it's spying for Persia." He turned to Suren. "You're under arrest for the same reasons and your property is impounded as evidence." Then he pushed them out the door and into the street.

Meherdates and Suren exchanged frightened looks and the priest looked wildly around the street, seeking help. They were led away quickly, but a crowd had gathered and someone from the crowd turned, ran down the street and entered the Temple of Mithra.

XXIII

SUREN AND MEHERDATES ARE QUESTIONED IN COURT

The array of judicial officers in the courtroom was very impressive. Judge Carbo, the local Puteoli magistrate who had signed the order to open the safe deposit box, sat in the middle of the raised tribunal. Judge Herminius was on his right and Judge Severus on his left. Clerks, assessors and aides sat on the sides and behind the judges, crowding the tribunal area. Lictors with bundles of rods and axes lined the walls.

They had decided to question Suren, the priest of Mithra, first. The prisoner was led by two court officers to stand alone in front of the tribunal. All spectators had been cleared from the court.

Judge Carbo opened the questioning. In contrast to Judges Herminius and Severus, Carbo was a small man, rounded and balding. He had a full beard, lively brown eyes and a booming voice.

"You have a choice," Carbo addressed the priest. "You can confess to everything you know about the murders of General Cyclops, the police agent Publius Bassianus, Procurator T. Vibius Galba and the lawyer Ambibulus. Otherwise, we will immediately turn you over to the *curiosi* as a Persian spy. And after they finish with you, you will be sent to the arena *ad bestias* – to the beasts." Carbo smiled proudly at the two judges sitting with him, pleased by his opening question.

Suren was not so pleased. But he blurted out an answer, his body and voice shaky. His Latin was fairly good, but heavily accented. "I know nothing about any murders, *eminentissime*. I am just a simple priest of Mithra traveling through the Empire. I know nothing. I am innocent of what you say."

"What about the jewels and money in the safe repository. Do they belong to Meherdates or to you? "

"They are his, *eminentissime*."

"Then why were they in your name in the repository? How do you know him? Why does he trust you with these valuables?"

"I am his brother."

"His brother?"

"Yes. We are from Emesa in Syria and traveling together, he to sell jewels and me to see something of the world. We put our valuables in my name rather than his in the repository for safety. Nothing else."

"But your name is Persian, as is your brother's, are they not?"

"They are, but we are from the province of Syria, *eminentissime*. From the Empire. Not from Persia."

Severus turned to Carbo. "Let's hear from Meherdates then. He was the one who spoke to General Cyclops on the day of his murder."

"Meherdates to the tribunal," called Carbo. One prisoner was led out and the other led in. Meherdates stood before the tribunal.

"Name, status and city," commanded Judge Carbo in Latin.

"May I speak in Greek, *eminentissime*." He replied in heavily accented and broken Latin.

Judge Carbo looked at the other two judges. It was unusual, though hardly unprecedented.

"Name, status and city," commanded Judge Carbo in Greek.

"My name is Meherdates, *kyrie*. I am a free man, and a citizen of the city of Emesa in the province of Syria." His Greek was excellent, with only a touch of an eastern accent.

"What is your business in Italy?"

'I'm a seller of jewels. I'm on a business trip from my home city. I've traveled through Greece to Italy and I'm now on my way home by way of Antioch."

"Are you an army veteran?" asked Judge Severus.

"No, I've never been in the army."

Judge Carbo pointed a threatening finger at the witness.

"Why did you kill General Cyclops? Why did you kill Publius Bassianus, and the procurator T. Vibius Galba and the lawyer Ambibulus?"

Meherdates made a show of surprise and looked around in desperation. "There must be some mistake, *kyrie*. You have the wrong man. I didn't kill anyone. I don't even know who those people are, except for General Cyclops and I only met him twice."

"Twice?" boomed Judge Carbo. "Describe the meetings."

"I met him at the Blue Oyster Inn. In Baiae. I was staying there about a month ago. I met him at the gambling tables. The general heard I had jewels to sell and he invited me to his villa to display my gems. He said he wanted red stones, especially agates. I don't usually carry agates, *kyrie*. They're cheap stones. Occasionally I might have a transparent agate because some people think they're beautiful. But otherwise I don't carry them. That's all that happened the first time.

"The second time was when I went to his house to show him my jewels. I brought some rubies with me to show to the general because he said he wanted red stones."

"Did he buy any?" asked Judge Severus.

"No, *kyrie*. He became angry at me because I hadn't brought red agates. He started asking me questions about agates. He asked me if it was true that certain agates make athletes invincible when they go into a contest. I said I had heard such stories, but couldn't guarantee it. I didn't know. He then said he wanted to borrow all my red or vermilion stones. He said he was just going to boil them in a mixture of pigments to see if the mixture turned vermilion. He said it would only take about two hours. He had already prepared the mixture. If it worked, he said, he would buy the stones from me and pay triple the price. I could wait, he said. He would pay me for waiting, but it had to be that day.

"Naturally I refused, *kyrie*. I know he was a general, but I frankly didn't want him boiling my valuable rubies in vinegar or anything else. Who knows what could happen?" He shrugged his shoulders and opened the palms of his hands upwards.

"Go on," said Judge Carbo with a tone of suspicion in his voice.

"When I refused he got very angry and threw me out. That's the truth. I didn't kill him. I never even wanted to see him again. I swear. Let me take an oath before the gods. Any gods you choose, *kyrie*. Or all of them."

Judge Herminius leaned over and whispered into Judge Carbo's ear. Carbo gave a little laugh. Herminius then looked piercingly at the prisoner and asked a question.

"That night, a few hours after you argued with General Cyclops, he was murdered. And then, early the next morning, only a few hours later, you suddenly left the Blue Oyster Inn and disappeared. Explain that."

"I was scared," he answered. "After I was thrown out of General Cyclops' villa I returned to the inn. A few hours later I was visited in my room by the man who had the room next door. He said his name was Bassianus. He was very agitated and short of breath, as if he'd been running. He said he had seen me go into General Cyclops' house and then started to ask me a lot of questions about him. How long I knew him? Who his friends were? What did he want? When am I going to see him again? Things like that. He seemed to be in a hurry and didn't stay more than a quarter of an hour. But I decided to leave the inn the minute he left my room. I didn't like what I was getting myself in the middle of. So I packed my bag. But when I got half-way down the stairs, I saw General Cyclops coming out of the gambling hall. I thought he had followed me back, so I went to my room, locked the door, put the bed up against it and stayed awake all night. I left at dawn the next morning."

Severus interrupted. "Try to recall the conversation with Bassianus exactly. Did he say why he was in a hurry or what prompted him to question you?"

"No, *kyrie*. But he acted as if everything was urgent. As if something had happened. He mentioned a man with a limp."

"What did he say?"

"He wanted to know if I had ever seen General Cyclops with a man who limped. He wanted to know who he was."

Herminius asked a question. "When you left the inn, where did you go?"

"To Rome. That's where I've been until I returned here to take the ship to Antioch. It leaves on the Kalends. Tomorrow."

"Who is Suren? Why was your property put in a safe deposit box in his name?"

"He is my brother," answered Meherdates. "He's a priest of Mithra and wants to see the world, so he came with me on this trip. He can stay at any temple of Mithra wherever we go. It saves expenses. I keep my business assets in a box in his name to avoid..." — here he gave a weak smile — "...to avoid any unpleasantness or complications with...ah... the law." He didn't have to elaborate. All the judges knew the common practice of hiding assets, particularly from the scrutiny of the tax collectors or the courts.

"You told people at the Blue Oyster that you were going to travel around the Crater," said Judge Carbo. "Yet here you tell us you went to Rome. Explain that."

The judges began to grill him about the details of his story. "Going back to your first meeting with General Cyclops," asked Judge Carbo, "was anyone else present?" "On what day did it happen?" "Who else knew about the second meeting?" "At the first meeting, where were you physically standing? At the dice tables or at the 'Odds and Evens' tables or at some other game?" "What was General Cyclops wearing that night?" "What time was it?"

A message tablet was brought to Judge Severus by one of the court officers. Judge Herminius took up the questioning. "If the general asked you to bring agates to the second meeting, why didn't you bring agates?" "What did the general say was in the mixture he wanted to boil the rubies in?" "Why didn't you ask?"

Judge Severus untied the threads and read the message tablet. It was from the imperial mint in Rome. The three coins sent to them were definitely counterfeit! And there was a report attached along with the coins. There was no doubt. The coins were of a type known to the mint experts as having been counterfeited in Antioch during Hadrian's reign. The ring had been broken up, the report said, the factory discovered, the dies seized and the counterfeiters executed. But some of the counterfeit coins were naturally still in circulation and turn up occasionally. The message added that a mint expert was on his way from Rome with a full report and would examine all the coins when he arrived the next morning.

Severus closed the tablet, waited until an answer was completed and then asked Judge Carbo to call a recess. The judges, assessors, clerks and aides left the courtroom and gathered in Judge Carbo's chambers.

"I have a report from the mint in Rome," began Severus, pointing to the tablet. "It says that three of the coins found in Meherdates' safe deposit box are counterfeit. And I have reason to believe that Cyclops and Galba were connected with the ring that minted them."

"The Procurator Galba connected to a counterfeiting ring?" remarked Judge Carbo with surprise.

"You mentioned that to me a few days ago," recalled Judge Herminius. "Doesn't this mean that Meherdates got the coins from either Cyclops or Galba? If so, he's withholding important evidence from us."

"Let's ask him," said Severus.

They returned to the courtroom.

"Where did you first meet Galba?" asked Judge Herminius.

"Who is Galba?" answered Meherdates.

"The Procurator Galba," shouted Herminius. "The man living in the villa next door to General Cyclops. The man you also murdered."

Meherdates looked to Judges Carbo and Severus imploringly. "I didn't murder this Galba. I never even met him. I don't know who he is. What's going on here? What are you accusing me of?"

"And I suppose," said Judge Herminius sarcastically, "you also don't know Ambibulus the lawyer, another of your victims."

"I never met him either. I don't know what you're talking about. I don't know anything."

Judge Carbo had the bailiff show Meherdates the three counterfeit tetradrachmas.

"Where did you get these?" shouted Herminius.

Meherdates shook a little at the volume and tone of the question. "I never saw them before, *kyrie*."

"They were in your pouch in the safe-deposit box," Herminius accused in a harsh voice. "They're counterfeit." He voice was even harsher. "Where did you get them?"

"I don't know, *kyrie*," he said meekly. "I swear I never saw them before. I rarely examine the coins I get."

Judge Carbo now yelled at him. "Counterfeiting is a capital crime. If you don't start answering, you could end up as food for the wild beasts in the arena. Would you like that?"

Meherdates didn't like it. He was pale and frightened.

"I must have gotten them on my travels," he said. "Perhaps someone who bought my jewels. I have a list. You could investigate them. Let me see those coins again." He looked up hopefully.

Judge Carbo nodded. The bailiff held them in front of Meherdates' face.

"Yes. Now I recognize them," said Meherdates with a sudden look of recognition. "I remarked upon them at the time. One rarely gets three coins of the same exact type together, particularly older ones."

"Where did you get them?"

"I got them at the Blue Oyster, *kyrie*. At the gambling tables. I remember now. I thought they were lucky and I kept them."

Judge Herminius stared at him, stopped cold by the answer. Meherdates looked a little relieved. He was certainly clever, thought Severus. He could make up stories quickly and think under stress.

Herminius' tone turned sarcastic.

"Then, no doubt, you can describe the employee of the Blue Oyster who gave these coins to you?"

Meherdates made a show of thinking. "Unfortunately not, *kyrie*," he answered finally. "I have a bad memory for faces. But I remember it was at the dice tables. Of that I'm positive."

Judge Carbo called another recess.

"He's lying," said Judge Herminius when they reached chambers. "He didn't get those coins at the Blue Oyster."

"Perhaps we should torture him," suggested Judge Carbo. "I know he's not a slave, but there might be a loophole."

"There is," said Judge Herminius, thinking one up. "Three of the murder victims were government officials; a procurator, a general and a member of the imperial secret service. We could call it a plot against the government — and in wartime too. And he has a Persian name. It's obviously a treason case. And in a treason case we could use torture even on a Roman citizen."

"I'm opposed," interjected Severus quickly. "We have no evidence of any plot against the throne. And under the law torture is supposed to be used as a last resort. We wouldn't be conforming either to the law or the contemporary principles of *humanitas* if we ordered his torture.

"Besides," added Severus, "he's not lying about Bassianus."

"What makes you say that?" asked Carbo.

"Because his information solves the problem of who killed the *curiosi* agent and why."

"You mean this supports your theory about General Cyclops killing Bassianus?" said Herminius.

"Yes. It was General Cyclops. But I didn't know why until now."

"How did Meherdates supply the motive?"

"Don't you see what happened?" asked Severus rhetorically. "Bassianus was watching Cyclops' villa. He saw Meherdates go in and leave in the afternoon. Later he saw something else there. And it made him run back to the Blue Oyster and hurriedly question Meherdates about a man with a limp. Meherdates had been at the villa earlier and might know something about what just happened. Then, within a few minutes, Cyclops arrived at the Blue Oyster looking for someone. Who? Bassianus, of course. Why? To kill him. Because Cyclops had realized Bassianus had seen something he didn't want anyone to know. The general found the *curiosi* agent in the garden, perhaps by the fish pond itself, where he confronted him and killed him. Remember Bassianus was hit on the front of the head, so they may even have had words before Cyclops struck."

"But what did Bassianus see?" asked Judge Carbo.

"Cyclops spent the afternoon preparing himself for combat," replied Severus. "Even trying to resort to magic to make himself invincible, trying to obtain agates to boil. And I think Cyclops found combat not once, but three times!"

"Three times," repeated Judge Herminius. "Bassianus is one and Cyclops' own murder is two. What's the third?"

"The one Cyclops wanted the magic agates for. The one the *curiosi* agent saw. The man with the limp

Meherdates said Bassianus questioned him about. The one Bassianus must have seen Cyclops kill."

The two judges looked at him. "You mean Odysseus?"

"Yes. Odysseus." Severus said to them. "Don't you see? The Greek legends have been rewritten. In Baiae, Odysseus didn't kill Cyclops. In Baiae Cyclops killed Odysseus!"

SCROLL VI

XXIV

CYCLOPS' VILLA IS EXCAVATED

The digging started at Cyclops' villa early the next morning, while it was still cool. The idea, agreed to by all three judges, Herminius for Baiae, Carbo for Puteoli and Severus, was to look for a stash of counterfeit money, possibly buried by Cyclops somewhere on his property. Also, they hoped, if Cyclops had killed Odysseus, maybe he might be buried on the property as well.

Under the supervision of Vulso and Eclectus one work crew excavated the garden and grounds behind the villa, while another dug in front. Within a few hours the grounds looked like an army had dug earthworks and cavalry traps for a lengthy siege. While this was going on, Judge Herminius, on his own initiative, was off leading a renewed plunge into the hills to round up more suspects. Judge Carbo was in a courtroom in Puteoli. Judge Severus, however, was on the site, reclining comfortably on a couch inside Cyclops' villa, though his mind was in Lucian's *True History*, following the exploits of

Moon-ites, Sun-ites and their allies from the Milky Way and the Dog Star.

The excavations first attracted the children in the neighborhood and then a curious crowd of adults. By the third hour, *Vigiles* had to be assigned to keep the crowd off the villa grounds. The word had spread that something to do with the 'Odysseus murders' was going on and, with the arrival of food vendors hoping to cash in on a hungry and thirsty crowd, an atmosphere of a country fair developed among the bystanders. They all got a good laugh when Titus Mummius, the brothel keeper who actually owned the villa, personally came by in a desperate effort to stop the dismantling of his property. Vulso, however, simply kicked him off the grounds in full view of the crowd and told him to settle it in the courts. A little later the Town Councillor Gallicanus rode up in a large litter borne by eight town slaves and in an officious manner loudly demanded to know what was going on.

"Don't tell him," shouted someone from the crowd. "Kick him off too," shouted another.

Gallicanus, however, managed to get inside the villa and talk to Judge Severus. A short while later he strutted out imperiously, responding to jibes from the crowd by announcing that it was too secret to talk about. At about the fourth hour, just as the morning was beginning to get really hot and when some of the crowd dispersed to go swimming, there was a shout from two workmen in the garden. Vulso, Eclectus and several other police officers ran to see what had been found. One of the diggers stood by a shallow hole near a cypress tree, leaning on his shovel and wiping sweat from his face. He pointed into the hole. Vulso bent down and brushed some dirt away.

"Tell the judge," he said to Eclectus, "we've found a body."

Severus half-walked, half-ran from the villa and arrived at the hole at the same moment as the police doctor. The workmen cleared the remaining dirt from the body and the doctor jumped in and examined the corpse. A few minutes later he climbed out.

"It's a man," reported the doctor in an efficient tone of voice. "Medium build and height. Probably in his late forties. His throat was slit from ear to ear. It looks like he was ambushed from behind. By the amount of decomposition it looks like he's been buried for more than two weeks and less than two months. A safe estimate would be one month. He was probably killed around the Kalends of August.

"The remains of a plain, brown tunic he was wearing are also present. The only other thing I can tell you about him is that has a badly mended left leg bone, so it was once badly broken. He would probably have walked with a limp because of it. When I get him back to my office I can do a more complete examination."

The doctor walked off giving instructions to an assistant.

"It's definitely Odysseus." said Vulso. "The limp and the timing clinch it. Should I tell the workmen to pack up?"

"No." said Severus. "This shows we're on the right track. I want them to keep digging here. And now I also want to extend the excavations to Galba's villa." The judge walked back inside the villa smiling to himself and then resumed reading his book.

The word that a dead body had been unearthed had tripled the size of the crowd and by the afternoon they were gathered in front of both Cyclops' and Galba's villas. Lively gambling had been in progress for hours, with people betting on almost any conceivable contingency. Whether a second body or money would turn up next were the most popular bets. It was also becoming very hot and very hard on both the diggers and on the slaves of the onlookers. Some of the slaves were required to lift their masters, whether in litters, sedan chairs or on shoulders, and to keep them lifted for the best view of what was going on. One fat man had fallen asleep in his litter, but his six bearer-slaves weren't aware of it and continued to hold him aloft, sweat pouring down their faces. Finally, someone in front of them told the slaves and they lowered the litter, profusely thanking the man in the crowd.

Two hours after digging had begun at Galba's, a huge cheer went up from the crowd, interspersed with a few groans and curses. Word had come out that money had been found behind the procurator's villa. A new round of betting quickly got underway, while an iron strongbox was brought from Galba's garden into Cyclops' villa. It was opened in the presence of a mint expert who had arrived that morning from Rome. It took him a while to sift through 20,000 sesterces worth of gold, silver and bronze coins, but he pronounced them all genuine at first inspection.

Shortly after lunch another strongbox was discovered on Galba's grounds. There wasn't any doubt about the coins in this box either — they were all counterfeit and most were the same coin types as the three silver tetradrachmas found in Meherdates' safe-deposit box.

Severus turned to the mint expert. "Why would he keep these?" asked the judge. "The ring had been uncovered. Wouldn't it be dangerous to hold on these coins?"

The mint expert made a twisted smile. "Did you ever throw money away?"

"I never had counterfeit."

"It hardly matters. As long as they're buried on his property, there's little chance of the money being found by anyone. And it's easy for counterfeiters to convince themselves that the coins would be useful in an emergency. The workmanship on these coins is also quite good. They probably could be passed off fairly easily. After all, they haven't been in circulation for thirty years. And they can always be melted down into silver ingots."

"Did you bring the complete file on the counterfeiting ring that manufactured these coins?" asked the judge.

The mint expert produced a sheaf of papyri and handed them to the judge.

"There's not much to add to the initial report except that the ring operated for almost five years and the leaders were never caught. Only some lower echelon people, slaves and workmen, who were taken when the factory was raided. They were examined under torture, but somehow the report of their confessions, if they made any, seems to be missing. I don't know why." He pointed to one piece of papyrus. "That lists the names of those arrested and executed when the ring was broken up."

Severus scanned the list. It contained ten names. He passed the papyrus to Vulso. "Seven are unfamiliar, but you'll recognize three of them."

Vulso read them out loud when he saw the names. "Candidus...Gaianus...Herculanus." The centurion looked up. "The members of Cyclops' patrol are on this list."

Judge Herminius arrived in a litter in the late afternoon. The workmen were still excavating both villas. The mint expert was sifting through a thousand genuine gold aurei discovered in a third spot in Galba's garden. Vulso and Eclectus were inside the villa sipping iced white wine and exchanging army stories, and Judge Severus was back in the *aer* between the heavenly bodies.

"I received a message about your finds," said Herminius when he was received into the villa's atrium. "I hope you're now convinced that Meherdates got his coins from Galba. It connects them beyond doubt."

"How did your search of the hills go today?" asked Severus in response.

"I don't know. It got too hot and I went home, but it's still going on. However, it seems the arrest of Meherdates has put us into the good graces of the Town Council. I sent them a full report last night and this afternoon they sent me a bottle of old wine – a Nomentum — and a note of appreciation. I expect you and Judge Carbo got one too."

They were interrupted when one of the work crew was shown in.

"We've found another cache on Cyclops' property. It's being dug out."

Another workman was shown in carrying another strong box. He placed it on the table and a police officer went to work with a set of tools. In an instant the box was open. Severus pulled out a sheaf of papyri and started to look through them.

"What do you have there?" Herminius asked Severus.

"Personal papers, legal documents..." he replied as he stared at one of the sheets. "...and this." He read it intently.

"It's a confession," said Severus when he finished reading it. "Signed and sealed by the Procurator Galba. He confesses to his part in running the counterfeit ring."

"Why should he write such a document?" asked Herminius. "And why would General Cyclops have it?"

'I imagine," replied Severus, "that Cyclops forced him to sign it. It implicates only himself. This is what Cyclops held over the procurator's head, extorting money on the threat of making this confession public."

"Then this means," concluded Herminius, "that Galba killed Cyclops. He paid Meherdates to do it. Then Meherdates, in some dispute after the event, killed Galba and later Ambibulus, who probably knew of the arrangement."

"That's not the way it happened," said Severus firmly.

"It's not?" said Herminius. "How do you know?"

"Because it if were," replied Judge Severus, "Cyclops would not have taken pen and papyrus with him to the beach on the night he was killed!"

XXV

COCCEIUS

Judge Severus returned to his villa near Neapolis in the evening, had dinner with his *familia* and aides, and then suggested a relaxing evening of music. The judge tuned up his seven-stringed lyre and Artemisia took out her double flute and they entertained the household with a small concert. Severus, who had kept up his music since learning it as a boy as a required subject in school, played enthusiastically, and fairly well, while Artemisia was an even more accomplished musician. After a while, someone suggested songs and the master and mistress of the house played accompaniment for a medley of old and modern popular tunes they could all sing.

They were interrupted when Scorpus, the chief household slave, went to answer the door and returned to tell the judge that a young man named Cocceius was there to see him.

"Cocceius? I don't know anyone by that name," said the judge.

"He says he was the assistant to the lawyer Ambibulus and that you may remember him from court at the Galba hearing."

"Oh yes. I remember now. What could he want? You'd better show him in." Severus pulled the strap of the lyre over his head and set the instrument down. "I'll see him in the library."

When the young man entered the library, Severus recognized him. The judge motioned Cocceius to recline on a reading couch opposite the one Severus was reclining on.

"*Eminentissime*," began the youth hesitantly. He was a little nervous in the presence of a judge. "I'm Cocceius, the law assistant to the lawyer Ambibulus. You may remember..."

"I certainly do," said the judge. "I remember you from court. I'm sorry about Ambibulus and I'm trying to find his murderer."

"Thank you, judge. I hope you'll find out who did it." He paused. "That's why I've come. I've been thinking about it for days. You see, I don't know why Ambibulus was killed. I thought, perhaps, you might be able to explain it and then perhaps I could be of some help."

Severus was pleased. The young man might know a few of the secrets Ambibulus had hinted he was privy to. "Perhaps you'd like a drink. Some wine?"

Cocceius nodded. Severus called out to Scorpus who came running. "Bring some wine for us and some cakes and fruit. You'll have something to eat? Dessert?" Cocceius nodded again. Scorpus left to fill the order.

"Well, it's possible," said the judge, "that Ambibulus was killed because he knew or suspected who killed

Galba. Galba may have told him some things that pointed to the person who wanted to kill him."

"No, judge. That's not possible."

"It's not?" said Severus incredulously. "Why not?"

"Because Galba didn't confide in Ambibulus. I know because Ambibulus was constantly trying to pry information out of him and got nowhere. Ambibulus complained about it to me often. He would even use it as an object lesson for my legal training, telling me that clients who wouldn't tell you what they knew weren't as good as clients who would."

The judge sat up on his couch. "Are you sure, Cocceius? Didn't Ambibulus know Galba well? I assumed he did."

"Ambibulus had once done some legal work for Galba in Rome, having to do with business contracts and property claims. It was all very mechanical and impersonal. Galba only hired Ambibulus for your court hearing because he needed someone in a hurry. Ambibulus was at the Crater on vacation, and Galba knew him slightly. That's all there was to it."

"Cocceius," said the judge, "when I talked to Ambibulus the day before he died, he indicated to me that he had information to tell me about Galba, that he was willing to trade a favor for a favor."

"It's possible he knew some gossip about Galba's background. I understood that Galba wasn't as upright as his position implied. But I know that Ambibulus didn't know anything about these murders because Galba never told him anything. He avoided telling Ambibulus things. That's why I don't understand why he was killed. What reason could there be? He didn't know anything. So what motive would anyone have to kill him?"

"It's an interesting question, Cocceius."

Scorpus entered with a bottle of wine on a tray with two glasses and a bowl of fruit and cakes. He put them on a low table and poured wine for Cocceius and the judge. "A nice old Nomentum," said Scorpus as he poured.

Cocceius thanked the slave and drank down a glass thirstily.

"Now," said Severus, "I'd like to ask a few..." The judge stopped and stared at Cocceius. The young man was turning pale and ghastly. He clutched at his throat and tried to speak. He gasped for air and collapsed on the floor.

"Vulso!" yelled the judge. "Vulso," he screamed out the door. The centurion came running, with half the household after him. Severus pointed at the crumpled youth. "He drank some wine and just fell down."

"It must be epilepsy," said Scorpus with a worried look.

Vulso bent over the crumpled body. "It's not epilepsy. He's dead! What happened?"

"He just drank some wine," said the judge.

Vulso sniffed the wine bottle. "Where'd you get this wine, Scorpus?"

"It was in the kitchen," replied Scorpus. "On the table. I'll check."

Scorpus ran to the kitchen and returned with a young slave boy.

Glycon," said the judge, "did you bring that bottle of wine into the house?" He pointed to the wine on the table.

Glycon was frightened. He kept looking at the body on the floor.

"It was delivered this afternoon, *domine*. A slave said it was from the Town Council. That they had voted it to you for your help on the case, in appreciation of your services. I just thanked him and left the bottle in the kitchen. You were at the excavations and everyone else was out. I told Scorpus about it when he returned from the beach."

"What did the slave who brought the wine look like?" asked Vulso.

"I didn't notice," said Glycon. "He just made a little speech about the Town Council and left. I thought nothing of it and didn't notice what he looked like. He had a beard and wore an ordinary tunic, just like everyone. He might not even be a slave. I just assumed he was because he was making a delivery. I'm sorry, *domine*. I wouldn't recognize him, even if I saw him again. I'm sorry, *domine*. I didn't know."

Artemisia, Flaccus, Straton, Alexander and Proculus had all come into the library because of the commotion.

Vulso pointed at the bottle. "There's no smell, and obviously no taste. So it's probably arsenic."

Everyone turned to look at Judge Severus. They were all thinking the same thing. "I know," said the judge grimly. "It was meant for me."

"And you're not the only one," reminded Vulso alertly. "Judge Herminius mentioned it this afternoon. He and Judge Carbo received similar gifts from the Town Council. We'd better warn them immediately."

"What time is it now?" asked the judge.

Glycon ran to the atrium and checked the water clock. "The fourth night hour," he said when he returned.

"By the time a message could reach them tonight," said Severus, "they'd either be asleep or dead. I'll send the messages out at dawn. Vulso, you'll take one to Baiae and Straton can take the other to Puteoli.

"Meanwhile," added the judge looking at the body of Cocceius, "I don't want word of this to get out."

Severus turned to Vulso and Straton. He looked a little squeamish. "I'm afraid you'll have to bury Cocceius in our garden."

Severus never got to sleep that night. Even after everyone else was in bed, when all the oil lamps were out, he lay in bed thinking. Then silently, so as not to wake his wife, he threw on a light tunic and went outside. It was cold and the stars were ice bright. A brilliant crescent moon shone above the umbrella pines. In the distance he could hear the soft sounds of the wind and the surf. He paced back and forth on the grass until it got too cold and then he went back into the house. He fetched sulphur matches from the kitchen, lit the matches from a candle, then lit the oil lamps in the library, and resumed his pacing.

An hour later he woke up his court clerk. "Quintus," said the judge softly, "I'm sorry to disturb you, but I need something. Have you transcribed your notes of this case to date?"

Proculus rubbed his eyes and nodded affirmatively.

"I need them now."

Proculus got out of bed and opened a chest. He handed the judge several rolls of papyrus, one at a time. "This is the hearing at which Galba was questioned...This one is the conference with Judge Herminius' staff after Ambibulus' murder...Here's the notes of the in-court and in-chambers proceedings concerning Meherdates..."

"Thank you, Quintus," said the judge as he took the transcriptions. "You can go back to sleep now."

Severus returned to the library and began reviewing the notes. After a while he pushed them aside and began to think again.

"That settles it," he said to himself.

Then he wrote out three message tablets, melted some wax, and sealed them with his personal seal ring — a black hematite stone with an engraved trireme.

Before dawn the next morning, the judge entered Vulso's bedroom and woke him up.

"I have two message tablets for you take to Baiae."

Vulso rubbed sleep from his eyes. "Two? Who else besides Judge Herminius?"

"I also have one for the Town Councilor Gallicanus."

Vulso looked quizzical.

"Make sure you see them personally," added Severus. "Then wait for an answer and come back."

The judge then went into Straton's room, woke him up, and gave him a message tablet to be delivered to Judge Carbo in Puteoli.

Then Severus found Scorpus in the kitchen, discussing what had to be done that day with a few of the slaves. "Is someone going to the market this morning?" asked Severus.

"Yes, *domine*. Someone goes every day."

"Today I want you to go personally Scorpus and I want you to put another item on the shopping list. I want you to buy a dagger."

"A dagger?" said Scorpus with some surprise. "What kind of dagger?"

Severus thought a moment. "You know the type they use in sacrificing animals at an altar? A long one, with a sharp point."

Scorpus nodded.

"That's what I want," said the judge. "A sacrificial dagger."

Severus then went back to his bedroom, got his wife and children and went swimming for the rest of the day.

XXVI

A SOLUTION

It was a month and four days since someone drove a knife through General Cyclops' eye; it was two weeks since someone had shot an arrow through the throat of the Procurator Galba; it was eleven days since someone strangled the lawyer Ambibulus with a silver wire; it was the night after Cocceius drank the poisoned wine.

Judge Severus reclined on one of the reading couches in his library. The oil lamps were glowing and incense hung in the air. Judge Herminius and Judge Carbo occupied two other library couches, while the Baiae Town Councilor Gallicanus reclined on the pillows of a fourth. It was dark outside and everything was quiet and still. Only the rustle of the Town Councilor's toga as he shifted his position on the couch broke the silence.

"I intend to solve the Cyclops case tonight!" announced Judge Severus.

"You know who killed him?" asked Gallicanus.

"I know who killed Cyclops and Galba and Ambibulus and someone else as well," replied Severus, thinking of Cocceius as the fourth victim. "Let me tell you how I deduced it."

The officials looked at him in silent expectation.

"The keys to the case lie as much in the past as in the present. One key was in Judaea, at the court-martial trial of Cyclops. Another was in Antioch, in Galba's counterfeiting ring. And a third is in the events of this summer in Baiae. Common to each of these times and places are three individuals: Cyclops, Galba and a third person."

"What third person?" asked Judge Herminius.

"Galba's assessor at the court-martial, his governmental aide and counterfeiting partner in Antioch and the murderer of Cyclops, Galba and Ambibulus in Baiae."

Severus held up an open palm to ward off a flood of questions. "I'll prove it to you," he said.

"We all know the practice of a judge choosing his own assessor. Except in certain unusual cases," he nodded at Judge Herminius, "a judge always chooses someone he knows and whose opinion he values, like a colleague, a friend or an aide. Undoubtedly Galba chose his assessor at the court-martial in this way.

"We also know that both Galba and his assessor voted, against the evidence, to acquit Cyclops of desertion and that Galba was bribed. If Galba was bribed to render an unjust decision, so was his assessor.

"What was the bribe? A certain amount of money, of course, but there was even more. For after Cyclops was transferred to the northern frontier, Galba and a governmental aide turn up controlling the counterfeiting ring started by Cyclops and the members of his patrol who robbed the temple in Judaea. So a share in the counterfeiting ring was probably also part of the bribe. That being the case, it is obvious to me that Galba's bribed assessor and his governmental aide and partner in the Antioch counterfeiting operation were one and the same person."

"That seems right," said Judge Carbo after a moment's consideration. "But how do you know that he's now in Baiae?"

"Because," replied Severus, "Cyclops took pen and papyrus with him to the beach on the night of his murder; because Galba lied about him at the hearing and met him on the beach the night before he was killed and because Meherdates had counterfeit coins."

Severus sat up on his couch. "These are all explainable once we realize that the assessor is in our midst.

"Take Meherdates. Where did he get those counterfeit tetradrachmas? Not from Galba, if we believe the jeweler's story, because he said he never met the procurator. But he could have gotten them from Galba's partner in the counterfeiting ring who, like Galba, may have kept a cache of those coins.

"Consider Galba's conduct in this case. First he tried to hide his previous relationship to Cyclops, but when he realized I knew about the court-martial, he told us about the trial and even revealed that someone nicknamed Odysseus brought charges against him. But Galba withheld two pieces of information from me. One was that Cyclops was blackmailing him. Of course, it's easy to see why he would want that kept secret. The other fact he withheld was the identity of his assessor at the court-martial, though he surely knew it. Even if it's possible to forget the name of an assessor, Galba certainly didn't forget the name of his partner in crime in Antioch.

"So why would he keep his assessor's identity a secret? If he were dead or out of the picture, Galba would have given up his name freely and simply washed his hands of the Cyclops case. But he chose to protect his assessor's identity, despite the considerable pressure he was under.

"Then, the day before he was killed, Galba received a copy of a letter I wrote to the Urban Prefect in Rome, complaining about Galba's intransigence at the hearing and asking that the matter be brought to the attention of his superior, to the *curiosi* and, if necessary, to the Emperor himself. That night, Galba, still a nervous wreck, left a banquet early and met someone on the beach. After the meeting Galba felt relieved. But the next day he was dead.

"The conclusion is inescapable," said Severus, pointing a finger to emphasize the point, "that the burden Galba relieved himself of was the same matter he lied about: the identity of his assessor. And it is just as inescapable to conclude that the person he met on the beach was the assessor himself. Galba probably told him that he had changed his mind and would tell me who his assessor had been. That's why Galba was killed. The assessor didn't want me to learn who he was, so he silenced the procurator."

"Wasn't he afraid the assessor would kill him, just like he killed Cyclops?" asked Judge Carbo.

"If Galba had realized the assessor had killed Cyclops, he certainly wouldn't have risked meeting him and telling him about his change of mind. But Galba obviously didn't realize it. He thought Odysseus had killed the general. It was the natural conclusion for him to make when he learned, either from his daughter or from the court hearing, that Cyclops had seen Odysseus at the Crater."

"You mentioned Cyclops' taking pen and papyrus with him to the beach in the middle of the night," said Herminius.

"Yes. Why would Cyclops do such an odd thing?" Severus answered his rhetorical question. "The only reason he would take writing materials is so that either he or the person he met could write something. Yesterday, from Cyclops strongbox, I realized what the general wanted written."

Severus addressed the judge from Baiae. "Our clerks told us that Cyclops was extorting money from Galba. Yesterday we found out how he did it. Cyclops' scheme was daring. He forced Galba to sign a confession, admitting the crime of counterfeiting. Then he held the document over the procurator's head, like the sword of Damocles. Remember, Cyclops was safe from any counter-charges by Galba. He wasn't in Antioch when the counterfeiting factory was operating. He was far away, on the northern frontier."

"Now," continued Severus, "suppose the assessor, Galba's partner in the ring, were also in Baiae. Wouldn't he make a perfect second target for Cyclops' extortion scheme? And wouldn't Cyclops go about it in the same way, by forcing the assessor to sign a similar confession? It is therefore reasonable to assume that Cyclops met the assessor on the beach with the intention of forcing him to sign right then and there. The papyrus he took with him was the confession; the pen was for the assessor's signature!

"But the assessor," concluded Severus, "was made of sterner stuff than the procurator. Instead of signing, he took advantage of Cyclops' drunken state to kill him."

"But what about Ambibulus?" asked Town Councilor Gallicanus. "He had nothing to do with the extortion, the counterfeiting ring or the court-martial. Why was Ambibulus murdered?"

"Because Ambibulus told the assessor just what he told me. That he was an intimate of Galba's, knew his secrets and was ready to reveal them for a price. The assessor was afraid that I would buy them. Ambibulus was killed for the same reason Galba was — to keep him quiet. As it turned out, I've learned that Ambibulus was merely selling 'smoke', but neither I nor the assessor knew that at the time."

"When did Ambibulus meet the assessor?" asked Gallicanus.

"And when did he meet Meherdates?" asked Carbo. "When did he give Meherdates the coins?"

"Meherdates never met him," answered Severus. "As the jeweler first told us, he never saw those coins before. They must have been deliberately planted in the package that was in his safe-deposit box, after it was removed from the repository!

"And Ambibulus met the assessor the day after Galba was murdered. I know, because Ambibulus told me he talked to him!

"You see, I know who he is because only one person could have been misled, as I was, by Ambibulus' 'smoke' and also have had access to counterfeit coins and an opportunity to plant them in the package after it was removed from the safe depository."

"By Hercules!" exclaimed Judge Carbo. "Who is he?"

"Judge Carbo," replied Severus. "You had the opportunity to handle the package in Meherdates' box. You issued the court order."

Carbo looked shocked. "You're not suggesting that I put the coins in..."

Severus held up his hand. "You? Not at all, Judge Carbo."

"Gallicanus," said Severus. "You had an opportunity to talk to Ambibulus at the banquet, didn't you? What did he tell you about Galba?"

"Why nothing. Galba was there himself."

"Judge Herminius. You also handled the package from Meherdates' safe-deposit box. Judge Carbo first sent it to you and you had Eclectus bring it to me."

"That's right," answered Herminius defensively.

"And Ambibulus told me you interviewed him after Galba's murder, just as I did. What did he offer to tell you about Galba?"

"Nothing," snapped Herminius. "And I resent the implication." He looked at Carbo and Gallicanus for support. They were looking only at Severus, who addressed Herminius directly.

"Were you in Judaea during the revolt, Judge Herminius, or in Antioch at that time? Weren't you Galba's assessor at the Cyclops court-martial?"

Herminius stood up. "I'm leaving," he said. "This is an outrage."

"Sit down!" commanded Severus.

Herminius froze at the tone of Severus' voice and obeyed the command.

Carbo and Gallicanus stared at him, unbelievingly.

Scorpus entered the library with fruit and wine. He placed the bowl and bottle carefully in the middle of the low rectangular table and gingerly put glasses in the middle of each side, within easy reach of the couches.

"A Nomentum," said Severus, commenting on the wine. "A present from the Town Council," he added, with a smile and nod of his head toward Gallicanus.

Herminius went pale.

"Is this true, Herminius?" asked Judge Carbo. "Did you open Meherdates' package? Did Ambibulus offer you a deal? Were you the assessor at the court-martial and a participant in the counterfeiting ring in Antioch?"

But Judge Herminius wasn't listening. He was intently watching Scorpus open the bottle, mix the wine with water, and pour portions for each of the four men.

Then Judge Severus raised his glass in a toast. Judge Carbo and Gallicanus raised their glasses in unison. They waited for Judge Herminius, who, when he became aware of their glances, raised his glass in automatic response.

"To Odysseus!" toasted Judge Severus. "To Odysseus!" echoed Carbo and Gallicanus.

Judge Herminius' eyes shot wildly from Severus to Gallicanus to Carbo to the glass in his own hand.

Judge Carbo drank his wine.

Judge Herminius choked audibly and dropped his glass, spilling all his wine on the table and shattering the expensive glass.

"What's the matter, Judge Herminius," said Severus with an edge in his voice. Scorpus put another glass in front of Herminius and filled it.

"You look sick," said Judge Severus. "Look at him, Judge Carbo, Gallicanus, what do you think's the matter with him?"

"You do look pale, Herminius," commented Judge Carbo. "What's the matter? Can I get you anything. Slave," he said to Scorpus, "bring some water for Judge Herminius."

"Water won't help him," said Severus coldly. "He thinks the wine is poisoned."

"What are you talking about," said Carbo.

Gallicanus stared at Herminius unbelievingly.

"The wine was poisoned," said Judge Severus. "Someone drank it last night and died. Judge Herminius knows it was poisoned because he poisoned it. Judge Herminius was the assessor at the court-martial, a partner in the counterfeiting ring, and the murderer of Cyclops, Galba, Ambibulus and Cocceius. Isn't that right, Herminius?"

Herminius sat slumped on the edge of his couch, staring at the floor.

"I'm glad it's over," he said forlornly. "Cyclops was a brute. He would have ruined me. He told me he had just killed Odysseus and threatened to kill me too if I wouldn't sign the confession. He was drunk. He brandished the knife he had killed Odysseus with. I had no choice."

Herminius looked up helplessly. "Then Galba had no backbone. He was going to tell you about me. Then Ambibulus. I couldn't stop and it wouldn't end. The Town Council pressuring me. You closing in on me. It was a nightmare."

He slumped and held his head in his hands.

Judge Severus stood up and extended an arm toward Carbo and Gallicanus. "Come with me, Judge, Town Councillor." He escorted them out of the library and nodded to his slave Glycon who was standing just outside the door with a box between his hands.

Glycon took the box to the table and placed it in front of Judge Herminius. Scorpus took away the glasses and the bottle of wine. Glycon opened the box.

Judge Herminius was left alone with the sacrificial dagger.

An hour later, Scorpus and a team of slaves went into the library and cleaned up the mess.

EPILOGUE

MARCUS FLAVIUS SEVERUS : TO HIMSELF

A few days after I compelled Judge Herminius to kill himself, I took Artemisia to the stadium in Neapolis to watch the races. I thought it would be a day of mindless relaxation. But I was wrong, of course. There was too much on both our minds.

In the blazing midday sun, along with thousands of other spectators, we rose and applauded the presentation of the laurel leaf crown to the winner of the one stade race for boys. The fleet-footed youth acknowledged the cheers with a victory lap and then we settled down to munch our chick peas and await the one stade race for girls.

"What happened to Meherdates and Suren?" asked Artemisia, out of the blue.

"I don't know," I answered. "The *curiosi* took them into custody. If they're Persian spies, they will disappear. If not, maybe they'll be released. Maybe not even then. But I heard that the temple of Mithra in Puteoli was raided the other day by the *curiosi*, and the Father of the Temple in Puteoli, Zabuttas, was arrested along with all the other priests."

"Are they really spies?" She asked.

I answered truthfully that I didn't know. "Maybe they're a nest of spies and maybe they're completely innocent. The *curiosi* will decide by themselves and for their own reasons. No one may ever really know, except the people arrested and the *curiosi* and the *spasaka*. And they won't be telling anyone."

"I suppose," Artemisia said casually, "that if it weren't for you, Herminius would have gotten away with it completely. After all, before your assignment, he was in charge of investigating a murder he had committed himself. I'll wager his plan was just to attribute the murder of General Cyclops to a bandit lurking in the hills and let it go at that."

"Probably," I admitted.

"In fact," she continued incisively, "if you hadn't taken on the case, Galba, Ambibulus, Cocceius and Herminius would still be alive."

I hardly knew what to say, though the same thought had been troubling my mind.

"I didn't kill them," I answered her defensively. "Herminius did. And I didn't kill Herminius, he committed suicide."

She smiled at me in her knowing way. "Officially, yes. But we both know that a different reality often underlies appearances."

"Herminius was a criminal. So was Galba."

"That was thirty years ago. You dredged it up again. Everyone else had forgotten. They had reformed their lives. And Ambibulus and Cocceius were not criminals."

"What do you want me to do?" I answered. "I had a duty to investigate the case. I had a duty to bring all the relevant facts to light. I had a duty to find out who killed Cyclops. This is considered a virtue — *pietas, gravitas*. As it turned out I had an eel by the tail, as they say. How could I let go."

"When did you first suspect it was Herminius?" she asked. "I want to know. Was it before any of the other murders, or after?"

I was truthful. "When Galba withheld the identity of his assessor I began to think about who it could be and why he was concealing it. The idea that it might be someone at the Crater occurred to me. If that were so, even Judge Herminius might be a candidate."

"So you could have let go of the eel's tail then." She wouldn't let me off the hook.

"It was only a theory," I replied. "It might have been someone else — Odysseus, for instance. I didn't eliminate him until Vulso found out he was a cripple and that was after Galba was killed. And by that time Odysseus was already dead."

I then asked her "what would you have done in my place?"

"I would have told Herminius that I had a vivid imagination and suggested that he put any suspicions about him to rest. Diplomatically, of course. If he had never been in the East at the time, that would have ended it. If he had..."

"That's unrealistic," I replied. "I could not challenge another Roman judge in that way. It would have been an unforgiveable affront. Besides he probably would have lied about where he was thirty years ago. I wouldn't have gotten anywhere that way."

"Instead you ended up by driving him to desperation, to more murders and then to suicide. Was that a better result?"

Fortunately the herald announced the contestants for the next race and they entered the starting gates. I turned my attention to the field and the noise of the crowd picked up, making conversation difficult. When the race was over, Artemisia returned to the moral dilemma, but now she was understanding, supportive.

"I can't blame you," she said and squeezed my hand, giving me her special wry smile. Then she looked into my eyes for what seemed like a long minute and expressed my mixed feelings for me.

"You're in a type of arena when you deal with crime, and I know you have to fight your way through it. And then, well, when we push on one lever of human affairs, we can't always tell what it's connected to and what will happen. The consequences even of laudable acts are often obscure and sometimes tragic."

I love my wife. I felt understood when she said that.

So I solved the murder of General Cyclops. I also realize the process of solving it led to the deaths of Galba, of Ambibulus, of Cocceius, and even of Herminius. Some nights this can haunt me. But other nights, I can take out my *diopter* viewing instrument and look at the stars and the Universe, untroubled and with wonder.

Made in United States
North Haven, CT
16 April 2022